THE ANGEL
WITHIN

—·—

ROBERT GREGORY THAYER

THAYER ENTERTAINMENT

This story was originally written as an independent feature film starring Kellyn Lindsay as Laura, Robert Nuzzie as Scotty, and Tim Weigand as Dr. Johnston, the psychiatrist. Made on a budget of just $4,000, the film has since been credited—through personal correspondence—with helping to save a few lives.

The film is available to watch for free at the link below or by scanning the QR code.

YouTube link:

https://youtu.be/XtpyMLe3BtQ?si=fDVrgMrsfq3VE5Zw

Due to the film's limited budget, not all of the scenes originally written into the script—and later included in the book—were able to be filmed.

Scan this Code to watch the film!

CONTENTS

1

LAURA'S LAST FLIGHT

T he sun dipped low over the wooded horizon, casting the world in hues of amber and crimson. The evening was thick with the sounds of life—the crickets chirped in a steady rhythm, frogs croaked from hidden pools, and the last calls of birds lingered in the cooling air. All of it formed a chorus that had sung each night without interruption, until a faint hum grew louder, drowning out the natural song.

It was the steady beat of an engine, drawing near, louder and louder, until it overwhelmed the night's chorus completely. A small aircraft, painted a faded blue, skimmed the treetops, its engine roaring as it hurtled through the twilight sky. Inside the cockpit, all twenty-two-years of Laura sat, her hands steady on the controls. Her blue eyes gazed outside of the cockpit but seemingly beyond the beauty of the view of the earth and sky. The setting sun cast long shadows across her face, highlighting the softness of her skin and blonde hair, the sharpness in her gaze. But her expression was distant, her eyes fixed somewhere beyond the horizon, beyond the immediate world around her. She did not look afraid, nor happy—just empty.

In the silence of the cockpit, voices echoed, harsh and unforgiving.

Her father's voice, laced with anger: "Why didn't you come talk to me?"

Her mother, bitter, venomous: "I hope you're happy. You've ruined me, you little slut."

Her father's voice again, colder, pleading: "Don't you know by now you can trust me?"

Her mother's rage escalating, cruel: "You think you can ruin my life, my marriage, and get away with it?"

The voices twisted together, each one biting into her like barbed wire. She winced, her eyes narrowing as she took a shaky breath.

Much later, as the sun sank behind her, leaving the world bathed in a cold, blue darkness. The moon rose in its place, a silver sphere that shone high above, casting pale light over the endless sea of trees below. Laura's hand reached for the small red knob on the instrument panel—the engine's mixture control. Her fingers closed around it, and, almost tenderly, she pulled it back. The engine sputtered once, twice, and then died, leaving only the rush of wind against the fuselage.

She exhaled, a slow, heavy sigh that was nearly drowned by the sudden descent. She nudged the control yoke forward, her hands steady as the aircraft tilted downward, plummeting toward the earth below. The wind howled against the cockpit windows, filling her ears, silencing everything else, even the voices in her head. The trees rushed up to meet her, their dark shapes growing larger, closer, as the altimeter spun wildly.

A hint of a frown crossed her face as she tightened her grip on the controls, pressing the yoke further. The dials glowed red in the cockpit, their frantic spinning an eerie contrast to her stillness. She was calm, almost serene, as if the roaring descent were nothing more than a quiet walk through the woods.

Below, the forest stretched vast and dark, the treetops illuminated by the pale moonlight. Through a break in the trees, the silhouette of the small plane was visible, cutting across the moon as it descended with unwavering speed.

And then, with a thunderous crash, the plane met the trees, its metal frame tearing through branches and foliage, the impact ringing out like a volley of cannon fire. The noise was sudden, violent, silencing the creatures of the night in an instant. The crickets stopped, the frogs quieted, even the rustle of unseen animals stilled.

A breath, a pause, and then, slowly, the night sounds returned, as if the forest were drawing a slow, cautious breath. Crickets resumed their symphony, the frogs croaked, and the world settled back into its rhythm, leaving the shattered plane hidden among the trees, its intrusion a brief, violent ripple in the forest's endless life.

2

DR. JOHNSTON

Laura sat in the psychologist's office, her slender form draped in a stark white hospital gown and a fresh cast on her broken leg. She looked small in the wheelchair, frail against the backdrop of the richly furnished room, yet her face was calm, devoid of any visible emotion. She gazed past the polished oak bookshelves, past the certificates and awards that hung in tidy frames on the walls, her stare distant, as if she were miles away from the softly lit office.

Across from her sat Dr. Johnston, a man in his late forties, with neatly combed graying hair and warm but piercing eyes. His gaze was gentle yet steady, the kind that waited patiently for answers. He wore a dark suit, crisp and unwrinkled, and he leaned forward, his elbows resting on his knees, his attention fixed entirely on Laura.

She broke the silence first. Her voice was low, almost as if she were speaking more to herself than to him. "That's all I remember about the crash."

Dr. Johnston nodded slowly, allowing the silence to settle for a moment before speaking. "What happened after the crash?"

Laura's eyes shifted, looking upward to the ceiling as though the answer might be hidden there. She drew in a deep breath, exhaled slowly. "I don't remember much," she said, her voice faltering, barely above a whisper. She clenched her hands in her lap, the knuckles turning white. "I woke up..."

Dr. Johnston waited, his gaze unwavering. "And?" he prompted, his voice soft yet insistent, a careful push, like one would give to a door just barely ajar.

She closed her eyes, her jaw tightening, a flicker of frustration passing over her face. Her fingers tightened on the thin fabric of her gown, and then, with a quiet exhale, she spoke again. "I woke up, and..." Her voice trailed off, and then she looked at him, her eyes holding a glint of something unreadable. "He was just there."

Dr. Johnston watched her, his expression unchanged, though a slight furrow creased his brow. "He?"

Laura nodded, her gaze shifting back toward that distant place beyond the walls of the room. She said nothing more, letting her words hang in the quiet, thick with things unspoken. Dr. Johnston waited, watching her carefully, but she remained silent, staring past him, as if her mind were reliving something he could only guess at, something buried and unreachable, hidden behind the layers of silence.

3

— · —

Scott

Laura lay sprawled on the earth, a slender figure lifeless in the morning light. The plane's wreckage lay scattered fifty yards behind her, twisted metal catching the first hints of dawn. Smoke rose in lazy tendrils from what remained of the fuselage, filling the air with the faint acrid scent of burnt fuel and charred earth.

From the edge of the trees, Scott watched. He hesitated for a moment, surveying the scene—wreckage, debris, and the crumpled form of a woman lying still on the ground. She was unconscious, her face half-buried in the dirt, one hand stretched out as though it had been reaching for something. He moved forward, his steps cautious, his eyes never leaving her.

Scott was young, no more than twenty-five, with a strong build and a face that might have been handsome if not for the thin, wary line of his mouth. He approached, then knelt beside her, reaching out a hand to check for her pulse. He felt the faint rhythm beneath his fingers, and his expression shifted, his movements becoming deliberate, confident. He'd done this before, he knew what to do.

As he lifted her head, cradling it gently in his lap, Laura began to stir, her eyelids fluttering, her breath coming in short, uneven gasps. Slowly, her eyes opened, and her gaze settled on his face, hazy and unfocused. She looked up at him, and for a moment, her lips parted as though she might speak.

Scott looked down at her, his mouth curving into a faint smile. "I guess you're not the pizza delivery person, are you?"

Laura's gaze sharpened, and a faint spark of irritation flickered in her eyes. She stared at him for a beat, her face expressionless, then rolled her eyes, almost as if annoyed by his words. And just as quickly, the spark faded; her eyes drifted closed, and she sank back into unconsciousness.

Scott looked down at her, a mixture of relief and worry etched across his face. He turned his head back toward the wreckage, the mangled metal a reminder of the violence that had brought her here. The morning was silent around them, the smoke from the plane's remains rising steadily, but his focus returned to the woman in his arms.

4

SCOTT'S CAMP

L aura stirred awake, blinking against the dappled sunlight filtering through the canopy. She sat up slowly, disoriented, looking
around at her surroundings. This wasn't the cockpit, wasn't the inside
of her plane—this was the deep woods. She took in the primitive camp,
the simple shelter of pine boughs, the rough bed of pine needles she'd
been lying on. Her leg throbbed sharply as she shifted, and she noticed
a makeshift splint strapped around her calf.

She glanced down, seeing that she wore only her black panties and
a white tank top with thin shoulder straps. Both shoes were gone. She
tried to stand, biting back a gasp as pain shot up her leg. She sank back
onto the bed of pine needles, clutching her injured limb.

Nearby, Scott stood ankle-deep in a narrow stream, his eyes narrowed, focusing as he aimed a long, sharpened stick toward a flickering
shadow in the water. He thrust the spear forward, the motion smooth
and practiced, but before he could see the result, a piercing scream
shattered the calm.

He dropped the spear, his head snapping toward the sound, and
bolted back to the camp.

When he reached her, Laura was clutching her leg, her face pale
with pain. Scott stopped just short of her, catching his breath, his face

flushed. "I wouldn't move that if I were you," he said, voice steady, though he was still breathing hard.

Laura looked up, eyes wide with distrust. She didn't recognize this man, didn't know his intentions, and his sudden arrival didn't ease her nerves. He dropped to one knee beside her, ignoring her suspicious look as he examined her splint.

"Your leg's broken," he said. "Not as bad as your airplane, though." He glanced at the scattered pieces of wreckage, then leaned over to adjust the splint. His fingers moved with a doctor's precision, but his hand slipped just above her knee as he checked for tightness.

Without thinking, Laura grabbed a loose stick beside her and swung, striking him squarely on the head.

Scott let out a sharp, pained yelp, jerking back. "Jesus," he muttered, rubbing his head.

"Stay away from me, you freak!" Laura snapped, eyes blazing.

Scott held up his hands in a placating gesture. "It's okay, it's okay. I'm not here to hurt you. I set your leg as best I could while you were out." He leaned back, giving her space, then fished a canteen from his belt, twisting off the cap. He brought it to her lips, but she turned her head away, her face tight with suspicion. Scott sighed, setting the canteen on the ground within her reach.

"If that leg sets wrong before we get you back to civilization, they might have to break it again and reset it." He said it evenly, watching her, and the horror in her eyes softened just slightly. "And I just hope it doesn't get infected out here."

Laura looked down, gripping her leg with a mix of anger and help-lessness. Scott gave her a sympathetic nod.

"Sorry about the pants," he added. "Had to cut them off to get to your leg."

She flushed, pulling her tank top lower over her exposed thighs, but Scott only smiled, unbothered by her discomfort. "Don't worry," he said, half-smiling. "I was going to be a doctor once. They don't allow us perverts."

The joke fell flat, but he still extended a hand. "I'm Scott, by the way. What's your name?"

Laura ignored his hand, turning her gaze back toward the forest. Scott waited a beat, then shrugged and withdrew his hand.

"Well," he said, unfazed. "I'm Scott. If you need anything, just scream again. I'll be down at the stream trying to catch us something to eat."

Laura dropped her head onto her uninjured knee, hands clenched, her body tense. Scott rose, giving her a nod before making his way back down toward the stream, muttering to himself, "What a piece of work."

When he was out of sight, Laura watched him go, then turned back to her leg, eyeing the splint and the small, neat bandages around her ankle and shin. She looked at the canteen, finally picking it up. She unscrewed the cap, wiping the opening with the edge of her tank top, then drank deeply, feeling the cool water soothe her parched throat.

The campsite was simple, everything around her improvised, crafted from what the forest provided. She noticed pieces of her plane—a twisted panel, a charred piece of fuselage—piled together near the edge of the camp. The rest was all pine, rough-hewn logs, and the occasional rustle of leaves in the breeze. She was utterly alone, surrounded by the indifferent wilderness, the only link to her previous world a few pieces of broken metal and the stranger at the stream.

She took another sip of water, feeling a pang of frustration as she looked out at the small river running below the campsite. She leaned back against the bed of pine needles, disgusted and helpless, and stared up at the trees above. The leaves swayed softly in the breeze, and as she closed her eyes, the sounds of the forest washed over her, lulling her into a restless sleep.

5

—·—

FISHING

S cott crouched by the edge of the stream, his makeshift spear in hand. The clear water moved gently around the rocks, a mirror for the canopy above. He hummed a silly tune, the kind he made up on long, lonely days. Every now and then, he'd spot a flicker in the water—a flash of silver darting just beneath the surface. He jabbed the spear down, missing each time, his song turning into a mutter of curses.

But finally, with one lucky strike, he felt resistance, and he lifted the stick to reveal a wriggling, glistening fish. He grinned, his face rough but youthful, taking a moment to admire his catch.

Later, back at camp, Scott sat by the fire, poking at the fish roasting on sticks over the flames. He sang another off-key song to himself, loud enough to keep the forest animals at bay. He couldn't sing, not by a long shot, but he liked the way the sound filled the empty space.

Across from him, Laura lay curled on the pine-needle bed, her face half-buried in her arm. He glanced over at her occasionally, singing even louder. After a moment, her eyes fluttered open, irritated by the noise. She shifted, brushing the sleep from her eyes.

"I have to go," she said abruptly, sitting up.

Scott kept singing, pretending not to hear. "I know. We'll work on that tomorrow," he said, still focused on the fire.

"No, I mean I have to go. Now."

Scott finally looked up, puzzled, but understanding dawned quickly. He smirked, ignoring her urgency. "Oh, you have to go," he repeated with a mischievous grin, letting her squirm a moment longer. "So... what's your name again?"

She glared at him, jaw clenched. "Michelle, okay? Now, please—what do I do?"

Scott grinned wider and sauntered over. "I'm Scott, Michelle. Nice to meet you." He gave her a quick, mock-formal handshake, then moved a pine branch beside her bed to reveal a small hole in the ground.

"Okay, just slide over, carefully, and, well—go for it. Cover it with some dirt when you're done." He stepped back, watching her.

Laura hesitated, clearly unimpressed with the arrangement but too desperate to argue. She scooted painfully toward the hole, giving him a hard look. "Leave."

Scott chuckled, amused. "Fine, fine." He turned away, gazing up at the star-strewn sky and shaking his head, his laughter echoing in the quiet woods.

"Do you have any tissues?" she called after him.

He paused and glanced back. "There's some scrap fabric from your airplane, just next to you."

"Oh," she muttered, embarrassed.

Scott waited at a distance until he heard her say, "Okay, finished." He strolled back, taking his place by the fire, and carefully pulled the fish from the flames. He broke off a piece, passing it to her with a grin. "Here you go. You'll need to eat if you want to keep up your strength."

Laura accepted it hesitantly, sniffing it before taking a tentative bite. Her face twisted in disgust at the taste, but she forced herself to chew. Scott noticed and laughed. "I could've been a chef, too, you know."

He launched into another song, this time crooning the Beatles' "Michelle." The joke seemed lost on her, though, as she quickly interrupted, wanting an answer.

"Where am I?"

Scott glanced at her, taken aback. "You don't know?"

Laura shook her head. "I was trying to fly to the beach this weekend."

"The beach?" he said, eyebrows raised. "You're at least four hundred miles from any beach—and a solid two hundred miles from anyone else, as far as I know."

She absorbed this with a barely disguised resignation, though the hint of despair flashed in her eyes.

"So, you're out here alone?" she asked.

He shrugged. "Was, until you dropped in. Why aren't people out looking for you?"

Laura looked away, clearly unwilling to answer. "I don't want to talk about it," she muttered. "I don't want to talk about anything with you." She put her hands over her ears, shutting him out.

Scott moved closer, kneeling a few feet away from her. He looked at her intently, his face softened by the firelight, but the irritation was there in his eyes.

"Listen, 'Michelle,' I didn't ask for you to crash into my patch of forest, okay? I could've left you there to rot, but here you are." He paused, letting his words sink in. "I'll get you back to civilization, but in the meantime, a little courtesy would go a long way."

Laura stopped chewing, her gaze shifting to the fire as if she could see something in the flames.

Scott pushed himself to his feet, his face unreadable. "Get some rest," he said simply, and then he walked into the dark, leaving her with the crackling fire and her untouched meal.

Laura watched him disappear into the shadows, her heart heavy. She took another bite, swallowing her pride with it, and stared into the fire, the embers drifting upward like stars into the vast, endless night.

6

DID YOU FEEL THREATENED?

The office was quiet, still. Laura sat across from Dr. Johnston, wrapped in the stiff, pale fabric of her hospital gown. The light in the room was soft but flat, casting a faint, muted glow on the walls lined with books, certificates, and a few carefully chosen photos that signaled Dr. Johnston's gentler side. But it was all white noise to Laura, who sat staring just past him, her eyes glazed and distant.

Dr. Johnston leaned forward, his voice low and deliberate, though he was watching her with a peculiar intensity.

"So, this young man—Scott, you called him?"

She nodded slightly, her gaze steady and unfocused.

"Yes," she replied, her voice quiet.

He took a breath, adjusting himself in his chair. "And it was clear, from the start, that he wasn't thrilled about you being there? I mean, he didn't... like you being there?"

Laura's face softened slightly, an almost imperceptible shift as her eyes found a point somewhere between him and the wall. "No," she said. "No, he didn't. Not at all."

Dr. Johnston gave a small nod, listening as if each word were a breadcrumb on a long, winding trail he was eager to follow.

"And at any point," he continued, his tone more careful now, "did you feel... threatened? Either by the situation or by being with him?"

Laura blinked, almost as if surprised by the question. She let a silence settle between them before she spoke, her voice steadier this time.

"He didn't want me there. I knew that much," she said, her words tinged with something that might have been sympathy. "I could tell he was... inconvenienced by me. But he did nothing but try to help." She paused, a slight frown crossing her face. "He never wanted anything from me. Just wanted to be left alone."

She seemed to drift back again, her eyes darkening as though caught in some dim and wild place. Dr. Johnston waited, watching her with a look that was both understanding and relentless, his pen poised over the notepad as he gently urged her onward.

7

WHY DID YOU LIE TO ME, LAURA?

Laura woke with a start. The air was crisp and cool, the early morning light filtering through the trees in pale, scattered beams. She took a deep breath, steadying herself as the remnants of her dream faded, but she flinched again when she saw Scott sitting just across from her, silent and staring. His face was unreadable, his eyes dark, holding something she couldn't quite place.

"Why did you lie to me, Laura?" His voice was calm, too calm.

She shut her eyes, trying to shake the grogginess, searching for an excuse that didn't come. When she opened them, he was gone. Just like that. Only the lingering question hung in the air, accusing and unanswered.

"Scott?" she called out, looking around, but the woods were still and silent. She closed her eyes in frustration and muttered to herself, "Shoot." She'd upset him again.

She glanced around the camp. Next to her, a small bouquet of wildflowers lay neatly, their colors vivid against the forest floor. Beside them were a wild peach and a handful of berries, left carefully within reach. She looked away, dismissing the quiet offering, and let the flowers fall, brushing them aside without a thought. The fruit and berries remained untouched.

Down by the river, Scott was alone, tossing stones absently into the water. His jaw was tight, his eyes focused on nothing in particular. As he watched a lone leaf drift by, he muttered under his breath, anger simmering just below the surface.

Back at camp, Laura lay back, resting her eyes, but her senses prickled. She opened them slowly to find herself face-to-face with a cougar, its eyes locked onto hers. It sat only a few feet away, its tawny coat blending with the dappled sunlight, tail twitching as it watched her with calm, predatory interest.

Laura's heart hammered in her chest as she whispered, "Umm... Scott?"

Scott returned to the camp, taking in the scene with a slow, amused smile. He ignored her plea and reached for an axe.

"Don't worry," he said over his shoulder, barely glancing at her, "She won't eat you. She's not that dumb."

A wild, guttural scream echoed from somewhere in the woods, and the cougar's ears perked. With a tense pause, the animal turned and bounded away, disappearing into the trees.

Laura exhaled shakily, gathering herself. "What are you going to do with that?" she asked, eyeing the axe in Scott's hand.

Scott cast a sidelong glance at the untouched peach and berries near her bedroll. "You're supposed to eat the food, not the flowers," he said dryly.

She tried to play it off, forcing a laugh. "Oops."

Scott's expression hardened, and he walked away without another word. She watched him go, frustration building. "Scott!" she called after him, her voice edged with desperation, but he didn't turn back.

In a small clearing, Scott found a sapling, its thin trunk and leaves trembling slightly in the morning breeze. He lifted the axe, swung it down hard, his muscles tense with each blow. "Take that, you ungrateful, stubborn... non-eating... witch!" he muttered under his breath, chopping through bark and wood with each angry word. The tree finally gave way and fell to the ground, its branches snapping in a final, small surrender.

He took a deep breath, momentarily satisfied, watching the tree lie still.

Back at the camp, Laura lay down, staring blankly up through the canopy, her vision blurred as a tear slipped down her cheek. The woods around her were quiet again, peaceful, save for the faint, steady beat of her heart, alone among the trees

8

IT WAS MADDENING

Laura leaned back in her chair, arms crossed tightly as if she were bracing herself. She let out a dry laugh. "Basically, I was the total bitch."

Dr. Johnston's eyes softened, and he allowed himself a small smile. "If you truly treated him that badly," he asked, "why did he keep trying to help you?"

She shifted, looking away. "I don't know. He was different. When he realized I lied about my name, he was hurt. And I didn't see why I should explain myself. Why I was... Michelle, not Laura."

Dr. Johnston tilted his head, studying her. "It sounds like, in that moment, you were focused on yourself."

She nodded slowly. "Yes, I was. That is, until I got... bored."

"Bored?"

9

YOU'RE A VIRGIN?

The fire crackled low as Scott crouched beside it, working a pair of fish onto a spit. He was drenched in sweat from the morning's work, face drawn and serious. He barely glanced at Laura as he knelt to arrange the flames.

"You know you really stink?" Laura said, scrunching her nose in mock disgust.

Scott looked up at her, his expression hard and unfazed. "Are you hungry?" he asked.

"Yes," she admitted.

"Then shut up and leave me alone," he replied, turning his attention back to the fire.

Laura held back a grin. She'd managed to get him talking again.

"Fish again?" she prodded, eyeing the cooking flesh.

"That's right."

"Is that all there is to eat out here?" She shifted, sounding almost like a child.

Scott looked at her with a raised brow. "You don't have to eat anything if you don't like it," he said flatly, going back to turning the fish.

She softened, sensing he wasn't in the mood. "I don't mean to sound so picky," she murmured. "I just wondered if there were, you know... chickens walking around out there."

Scott shook his head, adding some wood to the fire. "Quail, maybe a wild turkey or two. But no chickens."

Her eyes lit up for a moment. "I love turkey."

He gave no answer, focusing intently on the fish as they sizzled and smoked over the flames. Laura watched him, her eyes searching his face for any sign of warmth. She cleared her throat, trying again.

"Did you find my duffle bag in the plane?"

"Yeah," he said, flipping one of the fish, eyes not leaving the flames.

"Well, I have some soap in there," she added, voice low. "You should use it."

Scott didn't answer. He stayed crouched over the fire, poker-faced, ignoring her suggestion.

A few moments passed. Laura watched the flames lick around the fish, her stomach growling despite her irritation. She looked up at Scott, who was still refusing to meet her eyes.

"Think maybe today you could help me wash my hair?" she asked softly, almost pleading. "I don't feel too clean just sitting here."

He paused, giving her a brief, assessing look. "Maybe after dark," he said at last. "I want to keep working."

Her curiosity pricked up at that. "What are you doing out there?"

"Trying to build a raft," he said, "so I can get you out of here as soon as possible."

She blinked, surprised. "You know how to build a raft?" She shook her head in mild amusement. "I'm impressed, Mr. Man!"

"Yes," he answered, curt as always.

"Have you ever built one before?"

Scott didn't respond, but kept working the fish, his jaw set in determination.

"Well, I have," she added, leaning toward him with a smirk. "I was once a Girl Scout. Maybe I can help you out if you need some tips?"

Scott's face remained stony as he turned the fish again.

"When was the last time you talked to another person?" she pressed, her tone softer.

He let out a quiet sigh, finally meeting her eyes with a guarded expression. "Not long enough."

A pang of guilt swept over her as she held his gaze. "I'm sorry," she said, voice barely above a whisper. "For lying about my name. I didn't mean to hurt you."

He brought the fish over to her without a word, setting it on a flat rock by her side. She took the meal, smelling it cautiously before taking a small, reluctant bite. Scott sat back on his heels, watching her.

"Think you could find some fresh clothes for me, too?" she asked, half-joking, half-serious.

He shook his head, exasperated. "Tonight, after I bathe, catch your turkey, and wash your hair," he muttered. "Just eat."

She bit her lip, looking at him with a trace of earnestness. "Scott, please. Let's not be like this with each other anymore," she said. "I'm sorry for the way I acted."

Scott's gaze darkened. "Why are you here, Laura?"

Her face fell, and she turned her attention back to the fish. "I don't want to talk about that right now."

Scott didn't push. Instead, he let out a resigned sigh, glancing away to the forest. "You're... very beautiful, you know that?" he murmured, almost to himself.

Her cheeks flushed in surprise. She looked at him, caught off-guard. "You're only saying that because you haven't seen a woman in five years," she teased, smiling faintly.

But Scott's eyes held a sadness she hadn't expected. "Yes, I have," he replied quietly.

She raised a brow, trying to read him. "Oh, so look who's been lying now!"

He gave a short, humorless laugh. "I've got memories," he said, turning his gaze back to the fire. "And that's all I need."

She stared at him, taken aback. "You... You're not going to get, I don't know, horny and try to assault me or something, are you?" she asked, forcing a laugh.

Scott's lips twitched into a half-smile. "Hadn't thought of that," he replied, unamused.

She squinted at him, studying his face with renewed curiosity. "How can you survive out here, all alone?" she whispered, as if trying to understand. "No talking. No... women?"

His face darkened, the humor draining away. "I hate most people," he said, his voice low and bitter. "And I hate our so-called society." He paused, his gaze hardening. "And women..." he trailed off, looking away.

She smirked. "You're not gay, are you?"

He laughed, surprised, his eyes widening as he shook his head. "No, I'm not gay," he muttered.

"Do you hate me, then?" she asked softly.

He looked at her, holding her gaze with a fierce intensity. "I just said you're beautiful," he replied. "I wasn't trying to prove anything, and it sure doesn't mean I want to..." he trailed off, frustrated.

"Oh my God!" she interrupted, her mouth dropping open in mock horror. "You're... you're a virgin!"

Scott's face reddened. He stood abruptly, turning to walk away, visibly flustered.

Laura clapped her hand over her mouth, stifling a laugh, then called after him, "Scott! Don't go. I'm sorry!"

But he didn't turn back, disappearing into the trees, leaving her alone by the fire. Laura lay back, staring up at the canopy above, an amused, puzzled smile on her face.

She whispered to herself, almost as if she couldn't believe it. "Is he...?" Her voice trailed off, and she let herself wonder.

10

STRENGTH

D r. Johnston sat back in his chair, legs crossed, a faint smile tugging at his lips. His voice was calm and analytical, soft but probing.

"Do you think it's abnormal," he asked, "for a man his age to be a virgin?"

Laura looked down, shrugging as if the answer was obvious. "For a man? Yes," she said, almost dismissively. "I mean, he should've been with at least one person by now. He's not Brad Pitt, but he's not an armpit either." She smiled faintly, then looked off, as if seeing Scott's rugged face in the distance. "If he'd wanted me, I wouldn't have turned him away. And I think most women would see enough in him to... you know, give him a test drive."

Dr. Johnston raised his eyebrow, intrigued. "Did you find him attractive?"

"I wasn't thinking about that at first," she replied quickly. Her gaze drifted, and her voice softened. "I was mostly thinking about how stupid I was."

He nodded, sensing there was more. "And why were you out there, Laura?"

She looked at him, then down at her hands. Her fingers twisted together as she answered with a question. "Can you tell me?"

"Yes," he replied, holding her gaze firmly. "Did Scott know?"

A shadow of regret passed over her face. "No," she said. "But I think he was catching on. The more I got to know him, the more I realized how stupid I'd been."

Dr. Johnston tilted his head. "What do you mean?"

She sighed, her expression thoughtful, almost reverent. "There's just so much more to life than what we see on TV or in the movies or what we think we're supposed to do in our tiny circles." She paused, searching for words. "And yet, in those tiny circles, there's power too. I don't know." She shook her head, eyes distant. "It sounds ridiculous saying it out loud."

Dr. Johnston leaned forward, pen poised. "When did he find out about your suicide attempt?"

"Not for a while," Laura admitted, voice barely above a whisper. "I didn't want him to know what a mess I was. I mean, I barely knew him. Who tells someone they've tried to kill themselves right after meeting them?" She laughed awkwardly, looking embarrassed. "That's hardly a great first impression."

Dr. Johnston jotted something down, listening carefully.

Laura continued, her voice tinged with a sad humor. "Imagine me telling him, 'Oh, sorry for crashing into your backyard, by the way—I'm so messed up I can't even get dying right.'" She shook her head, eyes misting over. "That would've gone over great."

The psychologist observed her, his face softened by a look of empathy. "So," he said, "while you were there, you didn't think of trying again?"

Laura hesitated, then shook her head slowly. "I guess... I wanted to be as strong as he was."

Dr. Johnston straightened slightly, his gaze sharpening. "Strong? You call that strong?"

Her eyes flashed defensively. "Yes," she said quietly.

Dr. Johnston leaned forward, his voice a bit firmer. "Here's a man who hides from society, hides from people—and maybe even himself—in the woods. As you've described, every time a conflict arises, he runs. He's living a terribly lonely and cowardly life, Laura."

She looked away, brows knit, chewing over his words. Then she looked back, a quiet fire in her eyes. "No," she said firmly, "he's not a coward. He's living a beautiful life, away from all the garbage and corruption of our so-called society. He's there because he chooses not to be a part of it anymore."

Dr. Johnston regarded her, his expression softening. He could see that Scott, this shadowy figure in her story, was more than just a man hiding in the woods. He was something she both admired and yearned to understand.

11

— · —

GLAD TO HELP

The dusk settled over the camp, thick and quiet like the end of the world. The fire crackled, sending up occasional embers into the air. Laura slept soundly, her face relaxed, her breathing slow and even. The world around her was still, save for the distant rustle of the trees and the occasional hoot of an owl.

Scott returned to the camp quietly, his bare feet making little sound on the earth as he moved. His hair was still damp from the bath he'd taken in the river, the water droplets clinging to his skin and hair like ghosts. He didn't mind the dampness. He sat down beside Laura's bed, just out of arm's reach. For a moment, he simply watched her, taking in the peacefulness of her slumber.

A wild flower, picked earlier, lay in his palm. He set it gently beside her, its delicate petals catching the last of the daylight. He studied her for a long moment, then glanced down at the fire, where a small bird—quail—sizzled on the spit.

He worked without haste, his movements deliberate, seasoned by years of solitude. He flipped the quail, his face illuminated by the low glow of the flames.

Laura stirred slightly, her eyelids fluttering open. The sudden change in the light woke her fully, and she blinked into the fading evening. She stretched with a soft groan, as if the weight of the day had been forgotten in sleep.

"My God," she muttered, rubbing her eyes. "I can't believe it's dark so soon. What time is it?" Her voice was thick with sleep, still tethered to the dreamworld.

Scott glanced up from the fire, his face unreadable. "I have no idea," he replied, his tone low, matter-of-fact.

Laura shifted, her gaze settling on the bird roasting over the fire. She eyed it suspiciously, then broke into a half-smile. "You call that a turkey?"

Her voice was tinged with sarcasm, but there was no malice in it. Just a weariness that had begun to creep in.

Scott didn't even look at her. "No," he said, flipping the bird again. "It's quail."

"I've never eaten quail." Laura sat up, brushing the dirt and grass from her clothes, blinking away the remnants of sleep.

"It's good. You'll like it," Scott said, then, after a beat, added dryly, "It tastes like chicken."

Laura laughed softly, the sound light and free. It was the first time she'd laughed like that since the crash, and it caught her by surprise.

Scott rubbed his eyes, tiredness creeping into his bones despite his best effort to hide it. He wasn't one to show weakness, not even to her.

"Are you sleepy?" she asked, still amused.

"No," Scott answered quickly, then paused. "Not yet."

She took a deep breath, inhaling the smoke from the fire. It smelled familiar, earthy. She sniffed the air again, this time in his direction. "You smell better."

Scott didn't answer, but he didn't need to. He simply looked at her, the corners of his mouth twitching up in the faintest of smiles.

Laura smelled herself, then grimaced. "Woof. I don't."

Scott continued his work without comment, tending to the bird with careful hands. His silence was a kind of acquiescence to her remark, but there was no judgment in it.

"Did you find my things?" she asked, her voice quieter now.

Scott glanced over at her. "Yes. I'll take care of everything after dinner."

"Thank you," she said, her voice barely audible but sincere.

He nodded, keeping his focus on the fire, though he was aware of her watching him. They worked in their unspoken rhythm, each absorbed in their tasks.

After a moment, Laura spoke again, her voice softer, more reflective. "You know, no one's ever done so much for me. You really make me feel lucky to be alive." She paused, her words heavier now, tinged with regret. "I'm sorry I was such a bitch at first."

Scott didn't look up from his work, but he didn't need to. His response was quiet, but there was a slight shift in his posture as he acknowledged her. "Glad I can help you, Laura."

Their eyes met for a brief moment, a shared understanding passing between them. It was a fragile thing, born of hardship and honesty, but it was real. Scott smiled faintly, and Laura's smile mirrored his, tentative but genuine.

For the first time, there was peace between them. In the quiet of the woods, with the fire crackling softly between them, they sat, just two people, drawn together by fate. And for a moment, it felt like it was enough.

12

SPONGE BATH

The fire crackled low, its warmth casting long shadows across the camp. Scott worked silently, his body still aching from the day's labor, but he moved with a purpose. He lifted the small bucket from the fire, its weight a reminder of the hard work behind the simple task. He carried it over to where Laura sat, the quiet evening air settling in around them.

He held the bucket out to her, the steam rising in delicate tendrils, and nodded toward it. "Feel it," he said, his voice calm but steady.

Laura hesitated for a moment, her eyes narrowing slightly as she reached out, dipping a finger into the water. She pulled it back quickly, shaking her head. "No," she said softly, the word almost a laugh. "That's too hot."

Scott didn't argue. He placed the bucket back over the fire, letting the flames lick the edges of the metal. He knew it would take a little longer, but it didn't matter. He could wait. He always could.

"Give it another try," he said after a minute, his voice soft but firm.

Laura bit her nails nervously as she watched him dip the bucket back into the water. She was restless, her eyes flicking between Scott and the fire. She wanted to be clean, wanted to feel something other than the grime of the crash and the days in the wilderness.

When Scott handed her the bucket again, she tested the temperature with her finger. This time, she nodded, satisfied. "This feels better," she said.

Scott didn't speak as he poured the water gently over her head, letting the warmth cascade down her neck. Laura sighed, her breath catching in her throat. "Yes," she whispered. "This feels so good."

Scott took the shampoo from her bag, pouring a generous amount into his palm. His fingers worked it through her hair, massaging her scalp with delicate care. The lather formed in soft bubbles, and Laura closed her eyes, leaning into the touch. She let herself forget the past few days, forget the loneliness, the crash, the pain. In that moment, there was just the warmth of the water and the soft pressure of his hands.

"This is heaven," she murmured, her voice barely a whisper.

Scott didn't answer, his attention focused on the task at hand. He rinsed her hair with careful precision, then dried it with a small towel, his movements slow and deliberate. When he was done, he pulled a brush from the bag, and, without a word, began to comb through her hair, working through the knots with gentle strokes.

"I feel so much better already," Laura said, her voice full of relief.

Scott soaked a small cloth in the warm water and looked at her with a faint, unreadable expression. "This is a little something I learned in med school," he said.

Laura raised an eyebrow. "Behave yourself, Mister."

Scott looked at her for a long moment, then sighed, a slight grin pulling at his lips. "Have you ever had a sponge bath?"

Laura shook her head. "I can't say that I have."

Scott bent down, taking the wet cloth, and gently began to wash her foot, careful to avoid the splints. He worked his way up her leg, each movement methodical and precise. He was used to being alone, to doing things for himself, but in this moment, he wasn't alone. He felt her presence, her vulnerability, and the quiet intimacy that lingered between them.

"So," she asked, her voice steady despite the strange situation, "did you finish medical school?"

Scott paused for a moment, the question hanging between them. "No," he said, the word low, almost distant. "Blood makes me sick."

"Why did you go in the first place?" she asked, her curiosity piqued.

He didn't answer immediately. Instead, he continued to wash her leg, his hands steady. "My father, and his father, and his father's father were all doctors," he said finally. "I was told that's what I was going to be."

Laura looked at him, a new understanding flickering in her eyes. "You were the only son?"

"Was," he corrected her, his voice flat.

"He disowned you?" she asked, her voice quiet.

Scott's lips pressed together in a thin line. "Does anyone really own anyone?"

The question lingered in the air, unspoken but clear. Scott handed her a fresh shirt and a pair of panties, both retrieved from the wrecked plane. He didn't look at her as he did, but she could feel the shift, the awkwardness of the moment.

"You didn't pack anything else," he said, his voice gruff.

"I know," she said, the hint of a smile playing at the corners of her mouth. "I'm just giving you a hard time."

Scott paused for a moment, then glanced at her. "Here, you'll have to do the rest yourself. I'll get out of here."

Laura looked at him for a long moment, then shook her head. "It's okay. I don't have much under here to hide," she said, her tone playful but tired. "You don't have to leave."

Scott walked away, but as he did, he turned back, watching her with a careful, sidelong glance. Laura, with a quick motion, pulled the shirt over her chest, then dried off her skin with the towel. She covered her breasts with the fresh shirt, her movements deliberate.

"I may need some help with my back," she said, her voice low.

Scott murmured to himself as he turned around. "I may need some help with my front."

"What did you say?" Laura asked, her voice teasing.

"I said," Scott replied, trying to mask the faint tremor in his voice, "just cover up your front."

Laura smiled, her eyes playful as she lifted her body slightly, slipping the shirt down over her legs and pulling it into place. Scott's gaze lingered for a moment too long, but he quickly averted his eyes, turning to walk behind her.

He hesitated before gently running his hands over her back, the warmth of her skin beneath his touch sending a strange sensation through him. His fingers moved with careful precision, washing away the dirt and the tension from her back.

"That feels good," she murmured, her voice thick with relaxation.

"Does it?" Scott asked, his voice rough.

"Oh, yeah," she said, the word a breathless sigh.

As he continued to wash her back, Laura asked, "Have you ever touched a woman before?"

Scott froze for just a moment. He had touched women before, but not like this. Not in this quiet, vulnerable space. He hesitated before answering.

"A few," he said, his voice quiet.

"Like this?" Laura pressed.

Scott didn't answer right away. "Not really," he said finally.

"Are you a virgin?" she asked, her voice delicate.

Scott hesitated again, his hands stilling as the question sunk in. "Yes," he said, almost to himself.

Laura didn't react immediately. "It's no big deal," she said. "I'm just curious."

Are you?" Scott asked, his voice barely above a whisper.

"No," she replied, "I really wanted to save myself for marriage, but things just happen, I suppose."

Scott didn't speak for a moment, his mind caught between the past and the present. "How old were you?" he asked, his voice soft.

"Twenty," she said.

"Were you scared?" he pressed.

"Yes," she admitted. "He kept saying it was going to be okay."

"How was it?" he asked.

"Not so good," she said, her voice low. "I was really tense. But later on, it got a lot better."

Scott rinsed the rag in the bucket, the water murky with soap and grime, before returning to finish washing her back.

"Why haven't you been with a woman yet?" she asked, her voice probing.

Scott didn't answer right away, his fingers gently working the cloth over her skin. "I always thought that sex is something you do with someone that you love," he said.

"Have you ever loved someone?" she asked.

Scott's gaze drifted to the fire, his thoughts momentarily distant. "I thought I did," he said finally, his voice barely audible. "What happened between you and this sex god of yours?"

Laura's face softened. "He just wanted to get in my panties."

"The thrill of the hunt, I guess," Scott said quietly.

The silence stretched between them for a moment before he finished, his hands drying her back carefully. "All finished," he said softly.

"Not yet," Laura said, holding up the panties. "Can you help me get these over my bad leg?"

She pulled off her old ones, tossing them aside without a second thought. Scott froze. He hadn't expected this.

"Well?" she said, her voice teasing. "Close your eyes if you have to. Or come have a good look at me. I don't care. Just help me get something on."

Scott hesitated, but then moved toward her, his hands shaking slightly as he worked to slide the panties over her splinted leg. His embarrassment was palpable, but he managed to get them on her, his touch careful and shy.

When he was done, Laura smiled, catching his gaze. "I saw that," she said, a playful glint in her eyes.

Scott smiled, the moment passing with an awkward but genuine warmth between them.

"Thank you, Scott," she said softly. "I feel so much better now."

"Anytime," he replied, his voice low and steady.

13

— · —

IT WAS BEAUTIFUL

D r. Johnston sat across from Laura, his eyes steady as he watched her speak. His pen rested in his hand, the tip not quite touching the paper. He studied her, the way the light hit her face. There was something different about her today, something softer in the way she carried herself. Her voice was steadier too, the words coming more easily now. The flickering light from the window seemed to catch the curve of her cheek, and Dr. Johnston noted it, the way she glowed as she spoke of Scott.

"Your face glows more and more as you continue to talk about him," he said, leaning forward slightly, his tone neutral but observant.

Laura's eyes darted down to her hands, then back up to meet his gaze. She didn't smile immediately. Her lips parted as if she had something else to say but wasn't sure how. After a moment, she spoke, her voice low but clear.

"It does?"

Dr. Johnston gave a small nod. "It does. It must have been pretty romantic?"

There was a pause. The question hung in the air between them, thick like smoke. Laura shifted in her seat, her hands folded tightly in her lap, but the tension in her body seemed to ease as she thought of him.

"It was beautiful," she said finally, her voice quiet. "The innocence of Scott... It really gave me hope that there's good on this planet after all." She exhaled deeply, her chest rising and falling with the weight of it. "I didn't know if I believed that before."

She fell silent then, her eyes drifting somewhere distant, somewhere far away, her mind clearly back with him. Dr. Johnston observed her carefully. The change in her was undeniable. The guarded way she had come in, the sharpness in her eyes, was now replaced with something softer, something almost tender. There was warmth there now, not just in her voice but in the way she held herself, as if remembering Scott gave her something to hold on to, something that had been missing.

It wasn't just about Scott, Dr. Johnston knew. It was the way she was able to access the part of herself she had buried—perhaps the part she thought was lost forever. The part that still believed in something beyond the noise of the world.

"Do you think it's possible, Laura?" he asked quietly, his voice almost a whisper in the quiet room. "Do you think good still exists in this world?"

She looked at him then, the question settling over her. For a long moment, there was only silence. The kind that filled the space with more than words could. Laura's gaze softened, and for the briefest of seconds, Dr. Johnston thought he saw the faintest trace of something unspoken pass between them. A truth neither of them had yet put into words.

Finally, she spoke again, the answer as simple as it was profound. "I do now."

14

DID YOU SEE THAT?

The night air was cool, crisp against their skin, but neither of them seemed to mind. The stars stretched across the sky like scattered diamonds, pinpricks of light in the endless dark. The silence between them was deep, a quiet kind of peace that hung in the air, unbroken except for the occasional rustle of wind through the trees or the faint crackle of a fire still burning low behind them.

Laura and Scott lay on their backs, side by side, staring up at the heavens. The ground was soft beneath them, the earth warm from the day's sun. She had never noticed how clear the sky could be, how the stars could seem so close, almost within reach, when there was nothing around to distract her.

"Where were you born?" Laura's voice cut through the quiet, soft but steady. She didn't look at him as she spoke. Her gaze remained fixed above.

"Baltimore," Scott replied without hesitation, his eyes tracing the constellations. His voice was low, almost like a whisper, blending with the night. "You?"

"Saint Michaels," she answered, her words more reflective now, almost like she was speaking to herself. "A small town on Maryland's Eastern Shore. I was born and raised there." She paused, a faint smile tugging at her lips. "I'll always live there, I think. I love it in some weird way."

Scott turned his head slightly to look at her, the faintest shadow of recognition in his eyes. "I know where that is. My family moved to the shore when I was just eight."

Laura turned her head to face him, their eyes meeting briefly before she looked back up at the stars. "How old are you?" she asked, her voice still soft but with an edge of curiosity.

"28," Scott replied, no hesitation this time.

"Really?" Laura's voice rose slightly, a note of surprise in it. "You moved there the year I was born." She smiled at the thought, the coincidence of it. "When's your birthday?"

"July 25."

"You're a Leo!" she said, her voice filled with a quiet amusement.

Scott chuckled softly. "I guess so."

"I've never met a Leo before," she said, her words drifting on the breeze. "I'm a Gemini."

Scott raised an eyebrow, his expression thoughtful but unreadable. "When's your birthday?"

"May 29," Laura replied, turning her head again to glance at him. "You know, Gemini and Leo are supposed to be perfect together. In everything."

Scott was silent for a moment, his gaze flicking to the stars before he answered, "Do you believe in that stuff?"

Laura closed her eyes, the sound of her breath steady in the night. "Yes," she said, almost to herself. "Haven't you ever read a description about your sign and been blown away by how close it is to your true self?"

Scott didn't answer right away. He was still thinking about her words, the way she said them, as if she truly believed. He shifted slightly, his body relaxing into the earth beneath him, the crickets' song a soft backdrop to their quiet exchange.

"All of your good points and bad points explained perfectly," she continued. "It's kind of scary, actually. They also say there are only a couple of signs that are completely compatible with each other. Gemini is one of Leo's."

Scott was quiet again, letting her words settle in the space between them. He had never put much stock in those kinds of things, but the way she spoke about it—so sure, so unshaken—made him pause. He could hear the sincerity in her voice, and for a moment, he wondered what it would feel like to believe in something so absolute.

"I don't really believe in that stuff," he said finally, his voice steady, but with a hint of hesitation.

Laura smiled softly, her eyes still closed as she thought about it. "I don't really know if it's true or not. But it's nice to think that at least something is."

Her words hung in the air, unspoken truths lingering in the quiet night. She let the silence stretch, the comfort of it wrapping around her. The steady rhythm of her breathing grew slower, deeper. She was drifting now, the soft pull of sleep calling to her, but the warmth in the air, the stillness of the moment, made her feel safe.

Scott reached out, his hand finding hers in the dark, his fingers brushing against her skin. It was a simple gesture, but it held weight, a kind of unspoken understanding passing between them.

"Did you see that?" Scott whispered, his voice quiet, almost reverent. He gestured toward the sky, his hand still holding hers.

Laura's eyes fluttered open just in time to catch the brief flash of light—a shooting star streaking across the sky, burning brightly before disappearing into the dark. Her eyes followed it, her breath catching for a moment, as if the universe had just whispered something to her.

But before she could say anything, she was already asleep, her hand still resting in his. Scott lay there for a moment longer, watching her, the flicker of the firelight playing over her face. Then, slowly, almost as if he didn't want to disturb the peace they had found, he leaned over and placed a soft kiss on her forehead.

He rose quietly, moving away into the shadows, his steps light. But as he walked, he glanced back once more, his gaze lingering on her peaceful face. A small smile tugged at the corners of his lips.

Laura stirred slightly in her sleep, her eyes flickering open just long enough to see him move away. She didn't speak, but the smile that played at the corners of her mouth was enough. She closed her eyes again, the stars above watching over her as she slept, the silence of the night stretching out, endless and comforting.

15

— · —

Make-Up

The sun rose slowly, its light spilling over the mist-covered forest, painting the trees with a soft golden hue. The air was cool, crisp with the last remnants of the night, but the warmth of the new day was already pushing through. It was a still morning, one of those rare mornings where time felt suspended, as if the world had paused to breathe.

At Scott's camp, Laura woke slowly, blinking her eyes against the softness of the dawn. The world around her was quiet, save for the faint sounds of the forest—an occasional bird call, the rustle of leaves in the breeze. She stretched, feeling the stiffness in her muscles, then noticed the small, familiar gesture beside her. There, lying delicately next to her, was the fresh flower Scott had left for her, along with the small offering of berries and a ripe peach.

She reached for the peach first, her fingers brushing the soft skin of the fruit. It felt cool against her hand, a welcome sensation in the still warmth of the morning. Without thinking much, she sank her teeth into the flesh, the sweet juice dripping down her chin. She closed her eyes for a moment, savoring the taste, the simplicity of it.

In the woods, just beyond the camp, Scott was working on the raft, his back to her as he hammered at the logs with a rhythm that was almost musical. He was singing—low at first, then louder, with more energy—an old Elvis song, the words bouncing off the trees and the steady thud of his work. He didn't seem to care much about the task at hand, enjoying the sound of his own voice, lost in it.

The song ended abruptly, as something in the distance—a scream, wild and ragged—cut through the air. Scott froze for a second, his hammer held mid-air, his eyes narrowing as he turned in the direction of the sound.

He stood for a moment, listening, then shrugged as if the whole thing was a minor distraction. With a flourish, he placed his hands on his hips and, in his best Elvis voice, called out, "Thank you...ah...thank you very much."

He couldn't help but chuckle to himself before he returned to his work.

Back at the camp, Laura was sitting in front of her small mirror, working carefully at the task at hand. She was applying her makeup slowly, methodically, as if it were some ritual. Her fingers moved with practiced ease, brushing over her skin, her lips, though the makeup seemed almost absurd in the forest light. She knew it didn't belong here, knew it wouldn't change anything about the rough life she was living. But she kept doing it anyway, the old habit unwilling to leave her.

Scott arrived at the camp without making a sound, his footsteps soft on the ground. He watched her for a moment from the edge of the firelight, his presence unnoticed.

"I doubt that'll help you much," he said, his voice cutting through the quiet.

Laura didn't flinch at his words. She didn't even look up. Her hand continued its steady work, the lipstick slowly making its way across her lips. She had grown used to him, to his strange presence, but something about his voice irritated her now, a little more than it had before.

"I know," she replied, her tone dry, her focus unwavering.

Scott remained where he was, sitting on a nearby log, watching her. He didn't seem to care that he was interrupting her, or perhaps, he was just too distracted by the oddity of it all. He had never really understood the need for makeup in the first place, especially here, in the wild, in this place they'd made their own.

"You know," he said after a moment, his voice quiet but clear, "I really don't think you need makeup."

Laura finally stopped, her hand still holding the lipstick, but she didn't look at him. She kept her eyes on her reflection, studying the smooth, painted surface of her lips.

"That's not a good enough line, buddy," she said, her voice teasing but with an edge. "You'll have to try harder than that if you..." She turned her head then, finally ready to face him with a smirk on her lips.

But Scott was gone.

Her gaze flickered around the camp, confusion flickering for just a moment. He wasn't there anymore, had slipped away without a sound. She let out a frustrated sigh, her shoulders sagging.

"Scott?" she called softly, but there was no answer. Only the quiet rustle of leaves in the wind.

Her hand dropped to the flower that still lay beside her, its petals soft and delicate against her fingers. She lifted it to her nose, breathing in its fresh scent. It was the same flower he had left her every morning since they had been here. She closed her eyes for a moment, feeling the faint warmth of the sun on her skin, and let the moment wash over her, the quiet solitude of it.

The world was still, and for a moment, she could almost forget where she was.

16

GREG

D r. Johnston sat in his chair, leaning slightly forward, listening to Laura as she spoke. The chair creaked with each movement he made, but the silence hung in the air like something tangible.

"So you started to feel better as time went by?" he asked, his voice calm, almost soothing.

Laura's eyes flickered as she looked at him, the sunlight streaming through the window casting long shadows across her face. She took a breath before she answered, her voice steady, though there was a hardness in it.

"I felt like I belonged someplace for the first time in my life," she said, the words carrying a weight, as if she was still trying to come to terms with what that really meant.

Dr. Johnston nodded, taking it all in, but his next question came out like a gentle probe.

"You didn't think about your mother and father? How they were worried about you?"

Laura's lips tightened into a thin line, and she looked away, her gaze drifting to the floor as if trying to find something to steady her thoughts. Her voice, when it came, was low, almost resentful.

"They never seemed to notice that I was around. I really don't think they would miss me."

Dr. Johnston sat back, his pen moving across the page with a practiced hand. "Your missing plane made the national news. People were searching for you day and night."

Laura's eyes flicked up, sharp and quick. Her response was immediate, almost too quick, like a reflex.

"Well, you know they have to pretend they care when something like this happens."

Dr. Johnston paused, his expression unreadable. He had heard this before, but it didn't make it any easier to hear now. His voice remained steady, though, as he pressed on.

"You really think your mother and father don't care about you?"

Laura's hands, folded tightly in her lap, tightened further. She let out a breath, like she was trying to release something that had been stuck in her chest for a long time. Her words were edged with a bitter truth.

"Well, I'm their kid. They have to at least take responsibility. They're always too busy to talk to me, to answer my questions. They think I'm too old to be in the house and want me to move out on my own." She paused, as if thinking about something, her fingers twitching, a small, nervous gesture. "It's just... I don't like being alone."

Dr. Johnston tilted his head slightly, his voice measured. "Everyone has to learn to be alone before they can truly live with others. It's part of the process of discovering who you are... and developing boundaries to protect that person."

Laura stared at the floor for a moment, the words swirling in her mind. She had heard it all before, but it didn't seem to help, not really. Not the way she wanted it to.

"I tried," she said, but there was a hesitation now, a vulnerability that crept into her voice. "But now I'm scared after..."

Dr. Johnston leaned in slightly, his voice soft. "After what happened with Greg?"

Laura's head jerked up, her eyes wide, the name hitting her like a slap across the face. Her breath caught in her throat, but she didn't look away. Instead, she glared at him, a mix of disbelief and anger flashing across her face.

"You know about that?" she asked, her voice quiet but sharp, like a blade waiting to strike.

Dr. Johnston didn't flinch. He just nodded slowly. "Your parents told me everything they knew that might help me help you."

The words sank in like stones, settling deep in her chest. Her hands balled into fists in her lap, and her face flushed, the anger starting to rise in her once again.

"I can't believe they told you about that," she said, her voice low, the bitterness still thick in her throat. She blew a loose strand of hair from her face, her fingers trembling for just a moment.

Dr. Johnston looked at her, his expression unreadable. "Why?"

Laura's chest tightened, and for a moment, she didn't say anything. Her eyes darted around the room, as if she were looking for something to hold onto. When she spoke, her words came out in a burst, raw and unguarded.

"Because they promised me that they would never tell anyone anything about that," she said, her voice shaking now. "Again they lied. They really don't give a crap about me." Her hands flew to her face, burying her head in her palms. "I hate them. I really, really hate them!"

Her body trembled, the weight of everything finally coming to a head. She couldn't hold it back anymore. Not here. Not now.

Dr. Johnston didn't say anything. He simply sat there, listening, letting her words fill the space between them. He knew better than to say anything now. Some things could only be heard, not answered.

17

A CHALLENGE

The sun hung high in the sky, heavy with noon's heat, as Scott stood over Laura, watching her stir. The air was thick with the smell of fish cooking, the soft crackle of the fire beneath it. He stretched his arms out wide, his voice slicing through the still morning like a knife.

"Wake up, snoozer. You sleep all night, you sleep all day. It's fish time again."

Laura blinked, slowly coming to. Her body seemed to protest the movement, stiff from the night's sleep, but she pushed herself up with a stretch, yawning deeply. Scott caught a glimpse of her body shifting under the thin fabric of her shirt. His gaze lingered for a moment longer than it should have, before he turned his attention back to the fire.

"I'm so tired," Laura muttered, her voice thick with sleep. She opened her eyes, the light stinging against the fog of her exhaustion. The world felt blurry, like the edges of a dream slipping through her fingers.

She picked up the fish he had placed on a broad leaf, a makeshift plate beside her improvised bed. She chewed slowly, savoring the salty tang that spread across her tongue, letting it linger as if the taste itself held a story.

"How do you feel?" Scott asked, his eyes on her, not so much concerned but curious, the question an easy one that rolled off his tongue.

Laura looked up at him through tired eyes, her leg still swollen from the injury, the ache constant. "Besides the continual pain from my swollen leg and being bored out of my mind?"

Scott didn't answer immediately. He just stared at her. The words didn't seem to mean much to him, and maybe that was part of it, she thought. The ache in her leg was constant, but it was the monotony of the days stretching on like an endless river that was wearing her down. She was sick of looking at the same trees, the same dirt, the same skies.

"Why don't you draw or write or something?" Scott suggested, the idea casual, as though it were the simplest thing in the world.

"With what?" she shot back, her voice sharper than she meant. The silence between them grew, filled with the weight of their unspoken frustrations.

Scott didn't seem put off. Instead, he rummaged through his things and tossed a pad of paper and a pencil at her.

"I couldn't find a book, but I found the pad and pencil in the wreck," he said, a shrug in his voice.

Laura looked at the paper and pen in her hands for a moment, almost reluctant. "Thank you," she said flatly. She looked up at him then, trying to make out the lines of his face as he turned away, already back to his work. "Still building the raft?"

"Yes," Scott said, his voice distant, absorbed in something far away. "Why wouldn't I be?"

Laura didn't know how to answer that. She could have asked a hundred different things, but her mind kept returning to the same thought. She was growing impatient with the stillness of their lives, and with him.

"What's taking you so long?" she asked finally, irritation seeping into her voice.

"It's a big raft," Scott replied simply, as if that explained everything.

She frowned at him. "When do you think you'll be finished?"

"A couple more days," he said, not looking at her, but she could tell he was in no rush. "Why are you in a hurry?"

"I'm not," she said, her voice barely a whisper. "Just wondering."

The pause between them felt thick, stretching like the endless horizon. Scott was absorbed in his task, and Laura felt the urge to keep asking, to keep pushing. It was easier that way, to fill the silence with words instead of confronting what was really bothering her.

"Was it a girl that made you come out here to live?" she asked, her voice softer now, curious.

Scott didn't look up from what he was doing. "How's your fish?" he asked instead.

Laura blinked, taken off guard by the sudden change of subject. "Good as it gets, thanks," she said dryly, before adding, "It was, wasn't it?"

Scott didn't answer right away, and the stillness between them grew again, dense like the humid air of the forest. "Why do you want to know about this stuff?" he finally asked. "I think I know about you already."

"Know what about me?" Laura shot back, her voice sharp now.

"I know why you're here."

Laura felt a flicker of heat rise to her cheeks, but she ignored it, staring at the paper in her lap. "Stop trying to change the subject," she said, her voice quieter now.

"What subject?" Scott asked, his voice innocent, almost playful.

"Why do you live here?" she asked again, her eyes focused on the paper, tapping the pencil against the pad absently.

"Why not?" Scott replied.

She shook her head, the irritation welling up again. "I'll tell you what. I'll write down why I think you're here." She grabbed for the paper and pencil, ready to make a note, but Scott stopped her.

"Why?"

"Because I think you're full of doggie-pooh," she said, half-laughing, half-serious.

Scott frowned. "I just don't think you want to hear what I believe, that's all," he said, his voice lower now, the usual lightness gone. "You dream up your little story, and I'll tell you what I believe brought you here. Deal?"

"Deal!" she said, grinning now. "What do we get if we're right?"

"Nothing," Scott replied, his voice deadpan.

Laura raised an eyebrow. "No, we have to bet something."

"No we don't," he shot back, but she could see the glint in his eyes.

"I'll write down a wish, within reason, that I get if I guess your story right," she pressed.

"Oh, Jesus," Scott muttered under his breath, but she could see him thinking, considering it. He looked at her, then at the paper. She handed him the pen and paper, pushing it toward him.

"Write down your wish."

Scott hesitated, and she could feel the tension building between them. He didn't want to play along, but something in her made him do it anyway. Finally, he scribbled something quickly on the paper, folded it, and shoved it into his shirt pocket, the movement quick and sharp.

"Are you satisfied now?" he asked, his voice tired.

Laura took the pencil from him, smiling. "One thing you might need to know someday, Scott."

"What might that be?" Scott asked, his tone dry.

"Women are never satisfied," she said, handing him the paper again, her smile widening.

"Great," Scott muttered under his breath.

Later, Scott sat alone on the edge of the riverbank, a small cliff beneath him. His feet hung just above the rushing water, and his eyes, fixed on the distant horizon, grew distant. The afternoon sun slanted across the water, casting ripples of light that danced along the surface. He blinked, and for a moment, his eyes filled with something that made his chest ache. The tears didn't fall, but the weight of it was there, heavy and unspoken.

Meanwhile, back at the camp, Laura sat, her pencil moving across the paper as she wrote furiously. The silence between them felt thick, each of them wrapped in their own world, separate, but somehow together. The words she wrote flowed from her hand like an unspoken confession, like a secret she wasn't sure she was ready to face.

18

Turkey Baby!

Scott sat in the fading light of the campfire, watching Laura as she fiddled with the quail he'd brought. She looked around, her eyes searching for him, until he appeared from the shadows, revealing two freshly killed birds. The campfire flickered as Scott worked, methodical and quiet.

"You really were going to chicken out," Laura teased, but Scott didn't respond. His silence hung in the air between them.

He moved closer to the fire, pulling the feathers from the birds with practiced hands. There was something about his movements that made it clear he had done this many times before. Laura sat back, folding her arms, watching him without speaking. The firelight danced on her face, giving her a strange, almost ethereal look.

"Quail again, huh?" she asked, though it didn't sound like a complaint.

"Sorry," Scott muttered, not looking up. His attention remained on the task at hand.

Laura sighed, clearly tired of the silence. "Do you want to hear this?" she asked.

Scott looked at her, then at the fire. "I thought I was first?" he said, his voice thick with the weight of the day.

"That doesn't matter. Do you want to hear it or not?"

"I guess."

Laura smiled and began. Her voice, soft and measured, told the story she had crafted, a story about Scott's life. She recited it like she had memorized every word. There were no pauses, no hesitation in her delivery.

"On July 25, a baby boy was born. After much coin tossing, Mr. and Mrs..." Laura trailed off, looking at him expectantly.

Scott didn't reply at first, staring at her, wondering if she really wanted him to fill in the name. Then he sighed. "Walker," he said quietly.

"Walker," Laura repeated, writing it down. "After much coin tossing, Mr. and Mrs. Walker named their baby boy Scott."

The story continued as Laura described Scott's early years, painting a picture of a boy destined for greatness. The child was born into a semi-affluent family, raised with the idea that he would follow in the footsteps of generations of doctors before him. She painted a vivid image of a baby's crib lined with toys shaped like human body parts and a human skeleton doll that replaced the typical teddy bear.

Then came Scott at six years old, riding his bicycle down the street, only to fall and scrape his knee. Laura's voice shifted, turning playful as she described the small scratch that, in her mind, became a gushing wound. The scene was almost comical, with Scott's mother running to his aid in a panic, convinced that he was on the brink of death.

"His mother, not being a doctor, panicked and rushed Scott to the hospital for stitches," Laura said.

Scott couldn't help but smile at the exaggeration. It wasn't far off, he thought. He had never really gotten over the panic in his mother's eyes. They never spoke of it, but it had always stayed with him.

Laura's voice shifted to a darker tone as she continued. "Scott learned early on that he was to become a doctor, as all Walkers before him had. But it wasn't until medical school, when it was time to work on a real human corpse, that Scott realized he could no longer handle the sight of blood."

The words hung heavy in the air, and Scott shifted uncomfortably. He remembered that moment well, how his stomach turned when the professor unveiled the body on the table. The blood was like a flood, and Scott had found himself frozen, unable to cut, unable to look. He remembered how the other students had laughed when the blood splattered everywhere, how he had felt sick to his core.

But it wasn't just the blood. It was the weight of the expectation, the burden of his family's legacy that had forced him to question everything. He hadn't wanted to follow that path. The moment in the operating room had made him realize that he couldn't, wouldn't, do it.

"Cadavers don't bleed," Scott said abruptly, snapping back to the present.

Laura glanced at him, slightly confused. "They don't?"

"No," he said flatly, "they don't."

Laura, undeterred, continued with her version of events, her voice rising as she described how Scott had eventually left medical school. She spoke of the disowning by his father, of him being cast out of the family home. Scott listened, his mind drifting back to that moment when he was kicked out, when his father slammed the door in his face.

Scott had left with nothing but the clothes on his back and a car full of memories that weren't his to keep. He drove through small towns, searching for something. Anything. It wasn't long before he found Missy, standing outside a movie theater, her laughter carrying on the breeze.

But the Missy he had known was gone. The Missy he had thought was his future. She had changed, or maybe she had always been this way. He saw her with another man, a man who lifted her off the ground and kissed her with a passion that shattered Scott's heart.

He followed them, the jealousy bubbling inside him, until they stopped at a remote boat ramp. The air was thick with the sound of her moans, and Scott, hidden in the shadows, stood frozen. It was like watching someone die slowly, feeling the weight of the moment crush him. He couldn't look away, but he hated himself for it.

Laura's voice cut through the memory. "After a marathon hour of bliss, Missy and Tom finally finished and started to dress," she said. "Missy rolled down the window for some air."

Scott remembered the moment clearly. The heat from the car, the fogged windows, the sound of Missy's voice calling his name. The betrayal stung like nothing else.

"Why are you here?" she had asked, her voice cold. Her eyes had no warmth in them anymore. The ring she had given him, the ring that had meant so much to him, was nothing more than a symbol of a future that would never come to be.

He had thrown it away without a second thought.

Laura's voice trailed off. "She lied?" she asked quietly.

Scott nodded. "Yes."

The story had shifted now, the dark edge of his past surfacing in the light of the fire. It was strange, hearing his life laid out like this, like a story someone else had written. But it was the truth. The rest of it had been the same—his father's rejection, Missy's betrayal, his retreat into the woods.

"I guess we both win," Laura said, breaking the silence. "What did you wish for?"

Scott fumbled in his shirt pocket, pretending to search. "I must've lost it," he said, shrugging.

Laura raised an eyebrow, but didn't press further. "What about you?" she asked.

"I didn't wish for anything," he said, looking up at her. "I just want to see you get better."

Her gaze softened, and for a moment, the fire between them seemed to burn a little brighter.

Scott stood, stretching his legs. "You should get some rest," he said quietly.

Laura nodded. She didn't turn her head, but she knew he was gone. And for the first time in a long time, she wondered if she could stay out here with him, away from the world she had once known.

19

YOU WANTED TO STAY OUT THERE?

D r. Johnston sat on the edge of the chair, his elbows resting on his knees, watching Laura. She had been quiet for a while, the kind of silence that feels heavy, the air thick with the unspoken. Her face was pale, her eyes red from crying. She wiped at her cheek, her fingers trembling. He could see the pain in her. He could see it in the way she didn't look at him, but looked past him, somewhere far off, where things were different, where the world wasn't so cruel.

"So, you really wanted to stay there?" Dr. Johnston asked, his voice soft but firm.

Laura didn't answer right away. She sat on the opposite side of the room, her back pressed against the worn chair, her good knee pulled up close to her chest. The dim light from the single lamp threw soft shadows on the walls, but it did nothing to soften the sharpness of the air between them.

"Yes," she said, her voice barely more than a whisper. It wasn't an answer. It was a statement. A truth she had come to know for herself, even if she hadn't yet come to terms with it. Her head hung low, eyes gazing at the floor.

Dr. Johnston leaned back, his hands folded together in front of him. He watched her closely, as if trying to piece together the fragments of her, the way the pieces of someone's life don't always fit neatly together. He had seen people break before, but something about Laura made him wonder if she might never be whole again.

"Why?" he asked again, not to force an answer, but because he needed to understand.

She didn't answer him right away, but he saw her shoulders tense, the way her body stiffened. It was as if the question had opened up something inside her, something raw. Something she had been holding inside for so long that she couldn't keep it locked away anymore.

"Why not?" she replied, her words coming out like they were being pulled from somewhere deep inside of her. There was a bite to her tone now, a sharp edge, as if she were daring him to press her further.

Dr. Johnston let out a sigh, leaning forward just slightly, as if to make his presence known in the room. "Your family, Laura... Your friends..."

She finally looked up at him then, her gaze hard and cold, a look that seemed to pierce right through him.

"What about them?" she asked, the question hanging in the air between them like a challenge.

He paused, unsure of how to answer, and in that silence, he realized that there was a part of her that didn't want to hear the truth. The part of her that didn't care about her family's grief, about the people who loved her and were looking for her.

"I know how you feel," he said carefully. "But you don't know how a parent feels about their child. Especially when they're missing. The fear. The worry. The not knowing."

Laura's expression shifted, and for a moment, something flickered in her eyes. A kind of emptiness that she had been trying to bury.

"I know how it feels to lose a child," she said, her voice hollow.

There was a pause. A long, pregnant silence that stretched out between them. Dr. Johnston opened his mouth to speak, but no words came. What could he say? How could he answer her?

She had lost a child. He didn't know how deep that wound ran, or how long it would take to heal. He didn't know if it ever would.

"I'm sorry," he said quietly, his voice breaking the stillness, but there was no real comfort in his words. Not this time. Not for her.

She wiped her eyes, her face hardening again, as if she had built a wall around herself. She didn't need his pity. She didn't want it.

"I don't need your pity," she said, almost as if she could hear the sympathy in his voice before it even left his mouth. "I just want to be left alone."

Dr. Johnston stared at her for a long while, unsure if he could reach her. He knew that sometimes people needed time. Time to process, to think, to feel. But there was something about Laura that made him feel like time wasn't going to heal this wound. Not for her.

"You think I don't know what it's like to lose someone?" she asked suddenly, her voice low but filled with an anger that seemed to come from a place deep inside her.

He didn't answer. He couldn't.

Her eyes flared, and for the first time in what felt like ages, she looked directly at him.

"I lost my son," she said, her voice breaking on the last word. She looked away again, as if she couldn't bear the weight of her own confession. The pain in her eyes was unbearable. "I didn't get to keep him. And now... now, I can't even keep myself."

The words hung in the air, and Dr. Johnston felt the weight of them settle on his chest. He didn't know what to say, or how to make it better. He couldn't. There were no words that could fix this.

In the silence that followed, he understood. Some things couldn't be mended. Some wounds never healed. And sometimes, the only thing you could do was be there. And wait.

20

LAURA'S FEVER

The only sound was the soft rustling of leaves in the wind and the occasional creak of tree branches swaying in the dark. Laura slept, her body moving slightly as though she were caught in the middle of a dream, her breathing shallow, erratic.

Scott stood at the edge of the camp, the strange bluish light from the moon casting an eerie glow on everything around him. His figure loomed against the darkened trees, tall and silent, a shadow in the night. He watched her for a moment longer, his thoughts a mix of concern and something deeper, something he hadn't fully understood yet.

"Laura," he said, his voice cutting through the quiet like a knife.

She stirred slightly, her face contorting with the confusion of sleep.

"Laura!" he called, louder this time, his voice firm and insistent.

She jerked awake, startled, her eyes wide with panic. She blinked in the dim light, trying to shake off the remnants of the dream, her heart pounding.

"What? What's going on?" she asked, her voice thick with the fog of sleep.

Scott didn't answer right away. He extended his hand toward her, his fingers trembling just a little, but steady enough for her to notice.

"Come with me for a second," he said, his voice soft but urgent.

She didn't know what he meant, didn't know what was happening, but her instincts were telling her to follow him. She reached out, her hand brushing his as she took it. He pulled her gently to her feet, his touch firm yet tender.

"How?" she asked, still confused but trusting him more than she wanted to admit.

"Take my hand," he said again.

She placed her hand in his, and together they began walking. Their feet moved through the forest, the shadows of the trees stretching long across the ground in the blue light, their shapes warped and surreal. The trees themselves seemed to shimmer in the strange glow, their bark reflecting the pale light of the moon.

They reached a narrow path, and Scott led her toward the river. The water stretched out before them, smooth as glass, reflecting the night sky above. But it wasn't just the river. It was everything. The world around them felt different, like it was caught between two worlds, between the waking world and the dream.

Scott stepped forward onto the water, the cool surface rippling beneath his feet. Laura stopped, hesitating, looking down at the water, uncertain.

"It's okay," Scott said softly, his voice reassuring.

With a deep breath, she stepped forward, her foot touching the water's surface. It held her, firm and cool, and together, they walked. The air was thick with mist, the faintest trace of it clinging to the surface of the water. The trees lined the banks, casting long shadows, their leaves glowing with that strange bluish tint.

They moved deeper into the river, the water coming up to their calves, then their knees. Finally, they stopped in the middle of the river, the world holding its breath around them. Scott turned to her, his hands gentle on her arms as he drew her closer.

"This is so beautiful," Laura whispered, her voice filled with awe. She took in the mist swirling around them, the faint glow on the trees, and the way the water seemed to shimmer with a life of its own.

Scott's hand brushed against her face, his fingers warm against her cool skin. Slowly, he turned her face toward his, his eyes searching hers, as if looking for something he hadn't quite found yet.

"Will you dance with me?" he asked, his voice low, almost tentative.

Laura looked at him for a long moment, uncertainty flickering in her eyes. Then, a smile tugged at the corners of her lips, soft and shy. She nodded, a small, almost imperceptible movement, but it was enough.

They danced. Slowly at first, their bodies moving together with an awkward tenderness. But soon, the rhythm of their steps became smoother, more natural, as if they had always known how to move together, as if the world itself had bent just enough to allow them to fall into this perfect moment.

The mist curled around their feet as they moved, the world hushed, as if it, too, were watching them. The blue light made everything feel unreal, dreamlike, like they were suspended in a place that existed outside of time.

When the dance ended, they stopped, standing close, their breath mingling in the cool night air. Scott looked at Laura, his eyes searching hers, and in that moment, everything seemed to hang in the balance, as if nothing else in the world mattered.

He reached into his jacket and pulled out a small white flower, its petals soft and delicate. He placed it gently in the pocket of her jacket, his fingers lingering there for a moment longer than necessary.

"I know I don't know you very well," he began, his voice unsteady, "and I'm really not sure that I can trust you yet... but... well, if, for some reason, I could ever find the courage to once again offer a woman my heart... well... I would really hope that you would accept it."

There was a pause. His words hung in the air between them, fragile and uncertain. Then he gently rubbed the side of her face, his thumb tracing the curve of her cheek.

"Or at least someone like you," he added, his voice quieter now. "I really didn't believe someone like you existed anywhere."

Laura didn't know what to say. She wanted to say something, anything, but her heart was caught in her throat, the words escaping her. Instead, she did the only thing she could—she leaned forward and kissed him.

It started slow, tentative, but it quickly deepened, their lips pressing together with a hunger neither of them had expected. The kiss was soft at first, then more passionate, desperate, as if they were both trying to hold onto the fleeting moment, to something they couldn't quite grasp.

But just as quickly as it had started, Laura pulled away, gasping for breath. Scott's heart raced in his chest. He feared he had gone too far, too fast.

Then, from across the river, came the sound of a small voice.

"Mommy? Mommy?"

The words were soft, almost too soft to hear, but they cut through the moment like a knife.

Laura froze. Her face went pale as she turned toward the sound, her heart lurching in her chest. There, standing on the riverbank, was a small boy, no older than three. He was looking directly at her, calling to her as if she were his mother.

Laura's eyes welled up with tears. She stumbled backward, her hands trembling, and then, without a word, she collapsed into Scott's arms, sobbing uncontrollably. He pulled her close, his arms wrapping around her, trying to offer her some semblance of comfort, though he didn't know how.

"Why are you crying?" he asked, his voice gentle, confused.

The world around them felt like it had shifted again, as if it had turned upside down in an instant.

Scott sat by her side, still half-dreaming, his hand resting on her shoulder. "Laura. Wake up."

She stirred, gasping as she sat up suddenly, her chest heaving. Her eyes were wide, filled with the panic of a dream that wouldn't fade. She blinked, then noticed the cool denim jacket over her shoulders.

"Are you okay?" Scott asked, his voice low, filled with concern.

She nodded, slowly, as if coming back to herself. "Thanks. Yeah... I was just dreaming, I guess," she said, her voice thick with the remnants of the dream.

Scott reached into his pack and handed her a tissue. She took it, wiping her eyes, embarrassed, then blowing her nose.

"Thanks," she said with a nervous laugh.

Scott reached to touch her forehead, his fingers brushing against her skin.

"You're burning up," he said, his concern deepening. "I'll be right back."

He ran toward the wreckage, his feet moving fast, his mind focused on getting the supplies he needed. When he returned, he held a few rags in his hands.

"Now just lay back down and relax," he said, his voice calm, as he gently placed the jacket over her.

"I feel so cold," she murmured.

"You're running a fever," he said, his voice steady despite the worry in his eyes. He placed a wet rag over her forehead, gently smoothing it over her skin.

"You probably have an infection from your leg," he said. "Do you have any penicillin or antibiotics?"

"No," she whispered.

Scott moved quickly, wiping down her neck and arms with the cool cloth, trying to ease the heat in her body. She shivered under his touch, her body trembling as though the chill had taken hold of her.

Later, as the night deepened, Scott continued to watch over her. Her body shook beneath the covers, but she was still asleep, her breaths coming in slow, shallow gasps. He sat beside her, his heart heavy in his chest.

"It's okay," he said softly. "I'm still here."

Laura stirred, her eyes opening just a crack.

"Scott?" she whispered.

"I'm here," he said, moving closer.

"How are you feeling?" he asked, his voice low.

"Not so good," she answered, her words barely audible.

"You'll be fine. Just rest," he said, rubbing her arm gently.

She closed her eyes again, but when she opened them a moment later, there was something different in them. A kind of resignation, as though she were preparing herself for something.

"Scott?" she asked again.

"Yes?" he answered, his heart tightening in his chest.

"If I don't make it..."

"What?" Scott's voice cracked.

"If I don't make it..." she repeated, her voice stronger now, but still quiet.

"Yes?" he asked again.

She swallowed hard, her voice a whisper in the dark.

"You can have my airplane," she said, and then, a small smile tugged at her lips.

Scott smiled back, his heart aching at the bittersweetness of the moment.

"I don't want to go back, Scott," she said, her voice barely above a whisper. "Please don't make me go back."

A tear slid down her cheek, and another one followed from Scott's eye as well. He leaned forward, kissing her softly on the forehead, and held her close, the rag still resting on her forehead.

In the quiet of the night, with only the stars to watch over them, they both cried, for different reasons, but for the same unspoken fear.

21

—·—

YOU CAN'T REMEMBER?

The sun had just begun to climb over the horizon, casting a pale golden light across the forest. The trees stood tall and quiet, their branches still, the morning air crisp and cool. In the distance, the faint sound of birds waking in the trees echoed softly through the woods.

At Scott's camp, the first light of dawn filtered through the trees, revealing the mess of twigs and leaves where Scott had been sitting through the night. He was still there, his back against a large rock, his eyes half-closed but unblinking, his grip still tight around Laura. She was tucked against him, her body curled in an exhausted, feverish sleep. The fire had died down to embers, casting faint shadows on the ground.

As the sun crept higher in the sky, a breeze picked up, rustling the leaves and carrying with it the fresh scent of pine and damp earth. Slowly, Laura began to stir. Her eyelids fluttered, and then, with a soft groan, she stretched her limbs, stretching her arms above her head as if trying to shake off the weight of a bad dream.

She sniffed her arm and grimaced, the smell of sweat and dirt mixing with the faint smell of the forest.

"Whoof!" she said, pulling her arm away from her nose, her voice thick from sleep.

Scott chuckled softly from beside her.

"How are you feeling?" he asked, his voice still low with the remnants of the night.

Laura turned her head toward him, blinking as she slowly regained her senses. Her eyes were still heavy, but there was a lightness to them now. The fever had broken. She felt stronger. But the moment she realized just how stiff and sore her body was, she let out a small groan.

"Stinky," she answered, wiping a hand across her face, still trying to wake up fully.

Scott smiled, a small, private grin. "I thought you were going to die on me," he said, looking at her with a strange mixture of relief and something else—something deeper.

Laura stretched her arms and yawned, still groggy. Her mind was foggy, clouded by the remnants of a fevered sleep. Her throat was dry. She swallowed and looked at Scott.

"Were you up all night?" she asked, her voice weak but sharp with curiosity.

Scott leaned back slightly, stretching his long legs. He nodded, his gaze never leaving her. "I guess this means I don't get your airplane?" he said, a teasing tone creeping into his voice.

Laura blinked at him, trying to process his words. "What?" she asked, confusion clouding her face.

Scott leaned closer, looking down at her with a wry smile. "Last night, you said if you didn't make it, I could have your airplane," he said, his voice light, as if the words were a joke.

Laura blinked again, and then a laugh broke through her confusion. It was a small, disbelieving sound that felt strange in the quiet morning air.

"No way. I didn't say that!" she replied, shaking her head, her eyes wide with surprise.

Scott raised an eyebrow, clearly amused. "You really don't remember what you said last night?" he asked, his tone playful but gentle.

"No," she said, her voice still thick with sleep. She sat up slowly, stretching her neck and shoulders, trying to loosen the stiffness in her body. The world was coming into sharper focus now, but the dreamlike fog of the past hours hadn't quite cleared from her mind.

Scott chuckled softly, his eyes twinkling. "Oh yeah," he said, sitting up straighter. "I wanted to thank you for what you did, too."

Laura's brows furrowed in confusion. "What? You better tell me what happened," she demanded, still trying to piece everything together. She glanced at Scott, expecting an answer, but he only stood, stretching his arms overhead with a loud yawn.

He ignored her demand, the edge of a smile still tugging at his lips. "I think I'm going to get you some breakfast," he said. "Then I'll give you a bath. You need it."

Before she could respond, Scott was already walking toward the small firepit, his boots crunching softly on the dry leaves. His figure seemed to blend into the forest, his outline bathed in the soft morning light, his silhouette framed by the towering trees around them.

"Scott!" Laura called, sitting up more fully now, watching him. Her voice was a mixture of frustration and surprise. "You better get your butt back here and tell me what you are talking about!"

But Scott didn't look back. He kept walking, his long strides moving steadily toward the fire. His laughter echoed faintly over his shoulder as he disappeared deeper into the camp.

Laura growled under her breath. "He really drives me crazy!" she muttered, her voice low and filled with exasperation.

Then, without warning, she yelled at the top of her lungs. "SCOTT!"

Her voice ripped through the still morning, bouncing off the trees and sending birds scattering into the sky. The forest seemed to hold its breath for a moment, the echo of her scream hanging in the air.

Somewhere in the trees, birds burst into flight, their wings beating in a frenzied panic as they took to the sky. The sound of their departure mixed with the distant rustle of leaves, creating a chorus of wild, unrefined noise.

Laura rested her head in her hands for a moment. She let out a frustrated sigh and then looked toward the fire, where Scott had gone. His footsteps were fading, and she was left alone with the silence of the forest.

"Crazy man," she muttered to herself, a small smile tugging at her lips despite the irritation that still lingered in her chest.

The morning air felt sharp, the stillness broken only by the sounds of the woods coming to life around her. It was a beautiful morning, full of promise, but Laura knew she wouldn't let Scott off the hook so easily. She would find out what he meant, whether he liked it or not.

22

—·—

Do you want to make love to me?

Scott's camp sat still under the weight of the afternoon heat. The fire crackled softly as Scott stoked it with fresh wood, his movements deliberate but relaxed. He worked without hurry, his back to Laura as she sat on the ground, peeling a peach with careful fingers, the juice dripping down her wrist. She brought it to her lips and took a bite, her teeth sinking into the soft flesh.

Scott glanced over at her, his brow furrowing slightly. "How is it?" he asked, his voice low.

Laura didn't look at him. She took another bite. "It's fine," she murmured, not really answering.

Scott paused, a wisp of a smile tugging at the corner of his mouth. He took the bucket of water from beside the fire and placed it on the edge of the flames. The water would need time to warm up.

He wiped his hands on his pants, then looked back at Laura, watching her eat in silence. "What's that look for?" he asked, a teasing note in his voice.

Laura didn't answer. Her eyes narrowed slightly, but she said nothing. She simply turned her attention back to her peach, her eyes softening at the sweetness of it.

Scott waited for a response that didn't come, then sighed, reaching down for the bucket. He picked it up carefully, testing its weight.

"You gonna try it?" he asked, holding it out to her. "Feel the water?"

Laura shifted her gaze to him but didn't answer. She turned her back on him, a quiet defiance in her posture. Scott smiled, but there was a flicker of frustration in his eyes.

The silence lingered between them, thick and palpable, before Scott, without warning, dumped the water over Laura's head.

The shock of it made her jerk upright with a sharp scream. "That's cold!" she yelled, her face scrunched in surprise, eyes wide with indignation.

Scott looked over his shoulder, grinning. "Oh, too cold? I'm sorry," he said, feigning sympathy, though the amusement in his voice was unmistakable.

Laura, soaked and furious, glared at him. "Why did you do that?" she demanded, her voice tight with anger.

Scott walked back toward the fire, his grin widening. "I said I was sorry," he called, his back to her as he moved to warm the water. "I'm heating it up a little."

Laura gritted her teeth and stared at him, her frustration bubbling just below the surface. She stayed silent, the remnants of the cold water dripping down her face in tiny streams.

After a few moments, Scott returned with the bucket, offering it again, this time a little warmer. "Try it now," he said, holding it out to her with a quiet calm.

Laura eyed him, but the only thing that met her gaze was the playful defiance in his smile. She refused, crossing her arms in a show of stubbornness.

Scott set the bucket down, looking at her carefully. "You really don't remember what happened last night, do you?"

Laura blinked, her expression shifting from anger to confusion. "What happened last night?"

Scott hesitated, then shrugged nonchalantly. "Nothing happened, really. I was just messing with you."

Laura didn't believe him. "Nothing?" she asked, her voice laced with skepticism.

Scott sighed, the easy grin slipping from his face. "Nothing at all," he said, his voice steady. "I swear. I was just joking around."

Laura wasn't convinced. She stared at him, her lips set in a firm line. "You're lying."

Scott met her gaze without flinching. "I'm not lying, Laura," he said softly. "You're just looking for something to happen."

She turned her face away from him, biting her lip, then sighed heavily. "Maybe. I don't know," she admitted quietly.

Scott watched her carefully, then bent down to grab the rag from the water once more. He began to rinse it out, preparing to finish what he started.

"Do you want to make love to me?" he asked suddenly, his voice thick with uncertainty.

Laura froze. Her breath caught in her throat. Her eyes widened as the words settled between them. She didn't know what to say, her mind scrambling for a response that would make sense.

Scott continued, his tone lighter now. "I mean, I wouldn't be much fun. I've never been with a woman before, and I wouldn't know where to start."

Laura's face flushed, and she squeezed her eyes shut, as if trying to block out his words. She didn't answer him, but she felt a warmth rise in her chest, the weight of his admission sinking in.

Scott didn't press the issue, instead continuing to work his way down her back, the rag moving methodically over her skin. "I mean, I know what to do," he murmured, "but I wouldn't feel comfortable."

She kept her silence, but her lips quirked into a small, knowing grin.

"You always said you had to love someone to do something like that," she said suddenly, her voice soft but direct.

Scott's movements faltered for a moment. "Yeah," he answered. "I did say that."

Laura's eyes moved to him as he knelt down to wash her legs, her gaze following the movement of his hands with quiet curiosity.

"Are you ever going to leave this place?" she asked, her voice light, but with an undercurrent of something deeper.

Scott looked up at her, his face unreadable. "I don't know," he said, almost to himself. "Maybe not."

"Maybe you'll never meet another girl for the rest of your life, huh?" Laura pressed.

"That's very likely," he replied, his voice almost casual.

The moments stretched on between them, heavy with something unspoken. Scott dried her legs gently, his hands slow and careful as he worked. He handed her a clean tank top and fresh underwear. Laura slipped her old shirt off, not bothering to look at him, but she could feel his gaze on her.

She saw the way he watched her skin, his eyes tracing the curve of her body with an intensity that left her breathless, but she said nothing. He was slow to react, washing her chest, his hands tender as he moved downward. She closed her eyes, feeling the warmth of the water against her skin, and for a moment, she forgot everything else.

His hands lingered, and she shifted beneath him. There was a stillness between them, the weight of the moment almost too much to bear. She opened her eyes, meeting his gaze, her heart pounding in her chest.

"Did you really mean what you said?" she whispered, her voice barely audible. "About... about making love?"

Scott froze, his eyes locking with hers. He didn't answer, but she could see the hesitation in his face. The words hung in the air, unanswered, as the forest around them continued its quiet hum, indifferent to the turmoil inside them both.

Finally, Scott pulled away. He stood and walked off toward the fire, his silhouette fading into the darkening woods.

"Where are you going?" Laura called, her voice tight with frustration.

"I'm sorry," he said quietly, his voice carrying over the distance between them. "I just can't."

The silence that followed was absolute, deafening. Laura's heart ached as she sat there, alone once more, as the night closed in around her.

23

MAYBE HE WOULD LET ME STAY

"Did you offer to sleep with him?" Dr. Johnston's voice was measured, calm.

Laura shifted uncomfortably, but she did not look up. "Yes."

He paused, studying her. "Why?"

The question hung in the air, thick. She swallowed, eyes darting for a moment to the window as if searching for something outside. The silence grew heavy, but Laura spoke.

"I really thought he was cute," she said, her voice barely above a whisper. "The fact that I'd be his first... It kind of turned me on." She let out a soft breath. "I could've stayed out there forever with him. So, I was hoping..."

"Hoping what?" Dr. Johnston pressed, his pen tapping against the pad.

She glanced at him, her expression hardening. "I was hoping he'd fall in love with me," she admitted, the words raw and vulnerable. "And maybe let me stay."

Dr. Johnston nodded slowly, but he wasn't finished. "And what else?" he asked, leaning forward just slightly. "You didn't just want that, did you?"

Laura shifted again, hands now clasped tightly in her lap. She was silent for a long moment. When she spoke again, her voice was quieter, as though she was confessing something she hadn't yet come to terms with.

"I thought I might be the only woman he'd ever get the chance to be with." Her eyes flicked to his, defiant. "Maybe that mattered to me more than I realized."

Dr. Johnston took a long pause, watching her closely. "Do you think sex is a necessity in a person's life?"

She looked at him, caught off guard by the bluntness of the question. "Do you?"

He let the silence stretch between them, considering her response. Then, his voice broke it again. "Do you think sex is what he needed?"

Laura didn't hesitate. "Sex isn't a big deal to me," she said, her voice steadier now, though there was an edge to it. "I could do it with anyone—under the right circumstances. If they're clean, attractive, don't do drugs, don't smoke..."

Dr. Johnston's eyes narrowed slightly, but he didn't interrupt.

"Those things matter to you, then?"

"Yeah," she said, firm. "If they can't take care of themselves, how can I trust them to take care of me?" She shook her head as if to dismiss the thought. "Some guys, they just live to get laid. I stay away from them. I want something more than that. Something real."

"And what's real to you?"

Laura paused, her mind turning over something she had yet to put into words. "I like to have a relationship with someone first. Whether it's a friend who just needs to break a dry spell, or someone I could see long term... I like knowing I can trust them with my body and have fun at the same time."

Dr. Johnston raised an eyebrow. "A 'horny friend'?"

Laura's lips twitched, a small, rueful smile. "Yeah," she said, the words rolling off her tongue. "I would want them to do the same for me, without getting all serious. But at least we both know where we stand. I always thought I could trust a friend with my body... and have fun while doing it."

"How did you see it with Scott?" Dr. Johnston's voice was quiet now, but sharp.

She hesitated, her mind returning to the woods, to the firelight, to the vulnerability she had felt. Her eyes dropped again. "I thought maybe it could be a relationship," she said. "Sex can be more than just physical. It can be a way to bond, to draw two people together. But it needs emotion... it's not just about the act. It's about trust, about connection." She shook her head as if disappointed in herself. "I would have liked a relationship with him."

"How did it happen?" Dr. Johnston's voice was softer, but the question still hung in the air.

Laura closed her eyes, the memory still too fresh. But she didn't answer him right away. Instead, her mind lingered on the confusion, the loneliness, the way Scott had looked at her. He hadn't understood her. He never would.

The silence stretched.

24

I WANTED TO DIE

Scott lay on his back, shirtless, in the soft pine needles that covered the earth like a natural carpet. His arms were behind his head, and he was singing softly, almost lazily, "Afternoon Delight." The words echoed faintly in the stillness of the woods, interrupted only by the rustle of the leaves above. He stopped suddenly, his breath catching as a small shiver ran through him.

"Oh my God, Laura... that feels so good." His voice was hushed, a murmur that carried on the air, full of something unspoken. "There... oh yeah... that's it." His hand dropped from the air to something beside him, a strange creation nestled among the pine cones and grass.

He rolled onto his side, his body casting long shadows across the ground. The doll was crude—constructed from pine needles and grass. He had used the pine cones for the legs and tried to make the face as best as he could, though it was all imagination and no reality. The illusion was fragile, but it served its purpose. He grinned, a slight smirk on his lips.

"Baby, I'm going to do you like you've never been done before. And if I don't get it right the first time, well, baby, we'll just have to keep on trying."

The words were meant for Laura, but they were whispered to the figure he had made, the one that lay beside him in the fading light. His hands reached out, touching the doll. He slid himself on top of it, moving with a practiced, empty rhythm, his body arching in the quiet. The woods watched, silent and knowing.

Hours later, the soft, dusky evening air embraced him as he walked back to camp, humming the same song under his breath. The fish he had caught lay heavy in his hands. It felt like the right thing to do—fishing, singing, returning with something to show. But something was off, and he knew it.

Laura was waiting by the fire, her face unreadable. She looked up as he approached.

"No luck today?" she asked, her voice like a soft challenge.

Scott stopped, looking down at the fish in his hands. "Huh? Oh no, I was kind of busy today."

"Busy?" Her eyes narrowed. "What were you doing?"

His hands paused, the motion of preparing the fish halting as he thought about his answer. But he didn't give one.

"Have you thought about it?" Laura's voice softened, a question hanging in the air.

Scott's gaze darted around, pretending to focus on the fish again. "What?" he asked, though he knew what she meant.

"Never mind," she said quickly. But there was no mistaking the tension now.

"No, really. What?" He looked at her then, eyes searching, but something in his chest twisted uncomfortably.

She exhaled, clearly weighing her words. "Letting me be your first?"

The question landed between them like a stone thrown into still water. Scott didn't answer right away. He just looked at her, his face unreadable.

"I really don't think you'd want that," he said finally, his voice distant.

"How do you know what I want?" she shot back, her eyes steady, as though daring him to challenge her.

"I mean," he hesitated, eyes flicking to the ground, then back to her, "I don't think it'll be very enjoyable for you."

"It's not just for me," she said quietly, her voice holding something like resolve. "It's for you. I think you're very special, Scott, and I'd like to be something special to you."

The words felt like a weight on him, and he turned away, kneeling down beside the fire, his hands fumbling with the fish. His movements were quick, almost frantic, as if he was trying to distract himself.

"Forget about dinner for a while," she said suddenly, her tone sharp. "Come over here."

Scott froze, his breath catching as he turned to look at her. She was lying back on the ground now, her eyes closed, her body relaxed.

He stared at her for a long moment, caught between fear and desire. She patted the ground next to her, a silent invitation, and for a moment, it felt like time itself had stopped.

"I'm all yours," she said softly. "Do what you want, and please... take your time."

He didn't move at first, his body heavy with indecision. But finally, as if pulled by something beyond his control, he walked slowly to where she lay. The night felt cold now, the warmth of the fire distant, almost unreal. He sat beside her, unsure of what to do, his hands trembling just slightly.

"Follow your instincts, Scott," she whispered, her voice a soft thread in the dark. "Pick a place to start, and don't run away this time."

His heart beat louder in his chest. He looked at her—her body so close, so beautiful—and he felt like he was about to drown. "How is this going to work with your leg in the way?" he asked, his voice raw, unsure.

"If there's a will, there's a way," she replied. Her eyes were still closed, but she smiled, almost serenely, like she was at peace with everything.

He reached for her, his touch light and tentative. He kissed the top of her foot, letting his lips linger, feeling the warmth of her skin. Slowly, he moved up her calf, her thigh. Her breath hitched, a soft sound, but he didn't stop.

"That feels nice," she said, her voice low, and the sound of it seemed to settle something inside him.

Her leg was warm against his touch, and he could feel the tension in her body, though she seemed to relax under his hand. She moved slightly, pulling her shirt off, revealing more of her, and he looked at her, really looked at her for the first time, as if seeing her through a new lens.

She kissed him then, slow and deliberate, pulling him into something that felt fragile, yet real. She broke the kiss and whispered, "Just relax."

Scott lay beside her, his body uncertain. He didn't know what he was supposed to feel, what he was supposed to do. She kissed him again, and then, suddenly, stopped.

"I have to tell you something first," Laura said, her voice now serious.

Scott stilled, waiting, unsure of where this was going.

"Do you promise not to get mad?" Her eyes were closed, but he could feel her gaze resting on him, heavy with something he couldn't name.

"Why would I get mad?" he asked, though the edge to his voice betrayed his unease.

She took a deep breath, her hand resting on his as he caressed her stomach. The words came slow, almost hesitating.

"I haven't been completely honest with you," she said, her voice trembling now.

Scott's hand stilled, his fingers suddenly cold against her skin. His eyes flicked to her face, then down to the ground. There was something in her voice, something raw that made his stomach tighten.

"I didn't fall asleep, or get lost," she continued, her voice dropping to a whisper. "I really just wanted to die."

The words hung heavy between them, and for a long moment, there was nothing but the sound of their breathing. Her hand was at her head, as if nursing some invisible pain.

"I too felt like I didn't belong," she said, eyes still closed. "But now... now, I think I know why I'm alive. I'm glad I'm alive. I'm glad I met you, and I hope you'll let me stay here with you."

Scott's body stiffened, and he pulled away from her, standing up abruptly. He didn't know what to say, didn't know how to respond. He stared down at the fire, his face blank, and then without a word, he walked away.

"What are you doing?" Laura called after him.

He didn't answer, his hands working to prepare the fish again, his movements mechanical, as though he were trying to block out everything that had just been said.

"Not again!" Laura's voice cracked, frustration boiling over. "What's wrong?"

Scott didn't look at her. "I think we should just eat now," he said, his voice empty.

"I'm not hungry," Laura replied sharply. "What's wrong?"

But he didn't answer. He just continued, his back to her, as if she were no longer there.

"You know, I have some things to do," he muttered, turning away into the dark.

"Scott!" Laura's voice was sharp, desperate, but it faded as he disappeared into the night. Alone again, she picked up her shirt and pulled it over her head, feeling the weight of it, feeling the emptiness that was always just beneath the surface.

25

ELECTRICAL STORM

The storm had come on quickly, like a thief in the night. Dark clouds swallowed the moon, a heavy blanket that smothered the sky. Lightning split the air, the jagged streaks lighting up the trees, the ground, and everything in between. The first raindrops fell fast and hard, splashing on the earth, cool and heavy. They had the weight of a thousand promises broken.

In Scott's camp, Laura sat by the dying fire. It had been a good fire once, crackling bright and warm, but the rain was coming down in sheets now, and each drop hissed as it hit the flames. She hadn't moved. Her body was still, but her eyes were a storm of their own. Tears mixed with the rain that slanted down around her, soaking through her clothes, turning the earth beneath her to mud.

She had given everything. Her body, her words, her hopes. And now they were all gone, as if the storm had come just for her, to sweep it all away. The fire hissed and sputtered, gasping for breath, but the rain would have none of it. It was already dead, just like everything else that had mattered.

The roof of the small shelter above her didn't keep the rain out entirely, and a few errant drops fell against her skin, cool as they slid down her neck. But she didn't mind. The storm outside matched the one inside her chest.

She wrapped her arms around herself, as if trying to hold on to something that was slipping through her fingers. She didn't know how long she had been sitting there. It felt like hours, but maybe it was only minutes. She was numb. There was a chill deep inside her, colder than the rain, colder than the night.

Across the forest, down by the river, Scott stood on the cliff, his face tilted up to the sky, his eyes closed, letting the rain batter him. It wasn't cold; it was just wet, the kind of wet that seeps into your bones and never leaves. The lightning crackled around him, loud and violent, but he didn't flinch. He just stood there, drenched, his clothes heavy and clinging to his skin, his hair plastered to his face.

Tears mixed with the rain, running down his cheeks, but he didn't wipe them away. There was nothing left to wipe. No words left to speak. The storm was a fitting backdrop, like nature itself had grown angry, had taken on his pain.

Another bolt of lightning split the sky. For a second, it seemed as though the whole world had turned white, every leaf, every rock, every drop of water. Then the darkness returned, swallowing everything whole.

Scott breathed deep, his chest heaving as he let the storm wash over him. The rain wasn't kind. It didn't comfort him. It didn't heal him. But it was all he had left, all he could feel. And so, he let it come, let it take him under, let it pull him down into the earth where he could disappear.

26

I LOST A FRIEND

D r. Johnston sat back in his chair, the dim light of the room casting long shadows on his face. His eyes were steady, unblinking. He had asked the question, and now he waited, as if the answer was something he could measure, something that might explain everything.

"So, it never happened?" he asked.

Laura looked out the window, her gaze distant. The rain tapped gently against the glass, the world outside a blur of gray. She ran a hand through her hair, then let it fall back against the chair. Her voice was quiet, like it had been worn thin from too many words, too many nights of lying awake with this story.

"No," she said, the word almost lost in the silence. "When I decided to come clean with the reason I was there, he didn't want me anymore."

There was a pause. The air between them thickened, and the weight of the words hung in the room. Dr. Johnston didn't press her. He waited, letting her speak, letting her tell the story in the way she needed to. The quiet stretched on for another long moment.

"Interesting," he said at last, though it wasn't a word that fit the situation. It wasn't the word for something this raw. He hadn't meant it that way, but sometimes a word was just a word. It didn't make sense, but it was there anyway.

Laura blinked, once, twice, as though waking from a trance. Her hands were in her lap, clenched together, and she looked as if she might say something more but couldn't find the right words. Her lips pressed together for a moment, then she spoke again, her voice thick with the ache of the past.

"That night... I lost a friend," she said, her eyes lowering, her face turning away from Dr. Johnston's gaze. The words were harder this time, and they hung in the air with the heaviness of regret.

Dr. Johnston nodded, scribbling something on his notepad, though his attention was fully on her. "Did he say he didn't want to be your friend?"

Laura's fingers twitched, then rested still. She stared at the floor, the words coming slowly, like she was pulling them from the depths of something old and forgotten.

"He told me what he felt after I bothered the crap out of him..." She trailed off, as if the sentence itself had worn her out, and the rest of the explanation didn't matter anymore. She had pushed, and then he had pushed back, and that had been enough to sever whatever had been between them.

Dr. Johnston didn't ask anything more. There was nothing more to ask. The silence stretched again, filling the room with the weight of things unspoken. The rain outside had picked up, the sound of it louder now. It seemed to echo her words, the sadness in them. There was no going back. There was nothing left to fix. The friend was gone, and the night had taken him away.

27

—·—

I HURT YOU

Laura woke slowly, her body stiff from the night spent lying on the hard ground. She could still feel the coolness of the earth beneath her skin, but the warmth of the day had already begun to seep in. She pushed herself up, brushing the dirt from her clothes, but as she looked around, she saw that Scott was nowhere to be found.

Beside her, there was the usual spread—berries, a peach, and a bottle of water. No flowers today, though. It was a simple, bare offering, and it left her feeling like something had shifted in the air overnight. She hadn't slept well, had barely slept at all, really. The sounds of the forest had been too loud, too full of ghosts, and her mind had been full of other things, things she didn't want to face. She picked up the fruit and began to eat, the sweetness of the peach a small comfort against the heaviness inside her chest.

She chewed slowly, her eyes distant, her thoughts wandering back to the night before. It was hard to forget what had happened. She had tried to talk to him, to make sense of it, but he had shut her out. She wondered where he was now. What he was doing. If he even thought about her at all.

Scott was deep in the woods, working on the raft. His axe swung with a rhythm that had nothing to do with the task itself and everything to do with the anger that burned in him. The trees fell one by one, each chop more forceful than the last. The anger wasn't about the work, or the raft—it was about something else entirely. Something he couldn't name.

The sun hung high in the sky, its midday brightness harsh against the coolness of the morning air. He stopped for a moment, wiping his brow with the back of his hand. The sweat stung his eyes, and the pain in his chest had only grown since the night before. It wasn't something he was used to. He wasn't used to feeling this... undone.

He stood for a moment, letting his eyes fall to the ground. Then, without thinking, he began walking again, his boots crushing the leaves beneath him with a force that matched his mood. The love doll, the one he had made from pine needles and grass, lay in his path. He hadn't meant to leave it there, but now it was an object of something else—something worthless.

Scott stopped in front of it. The sight of it made his blood run cold, a feeling he couldn't explain. With a grunt, he kicked it hard, the pine needles and bits of foliage scattering into the dirt. He grabbed one of the pine cones that had served as a makeshift breast and threw it as far as he could, his arm feeling the strain of the motion. The doll was nothing now, no longer a symbol of whatever he had been trying to build. He had no use for it.

He turned and walked away, the anger still simmering beneath his skin. His hands were trembling, but he didn't care. He needed something to kill the feeling, something to make him feel anything other than the tightness in his chest. He pulled the small net from his pack, the one he had used to catch fish earlier. He walked to the stream and knelt, lifting the net to reveal a couple of fish caught in its weave. Without hesitation, he took a stick and beat the fish's heads, killing them with a quick and brutal motion.

When the deed was done, he stood and, without a word, began his journey back to the camp, the fish hanging from the stick in his hand.

Back at the camp, Laura sat by the riverside, staring at the flowing water as if it might somehow carry away her thoughts. The sky had begun to clear, and the sun was high now, but it didn't feel like a beautiful day. It felt like the calm before something else.

She heard Scott's footsteps before she saw him. He came into view, his form appearing like a shadow against the bright afternoon. His face was set, his eyes focused on something far off, something that had nothing to do with her. He didn't acknowledge her when he entered the camp. Without a word, he began to prepare the fish for lunch. The sound of his knife against the skin of the fish was the only noise between them. The crackle of the fire felt distant, swallowed by the tension in the air.

Laura watched him, trying to make sense of what had happened. She had wanted to reach out to him, to bridge whatever gap had opened between them, but it felt impossible. There was no way to cross it now. She took a deep breath and then looked down at the ground, thinking of something to say.

Finally, she raised her head and tried again. "Beautiful day, isn't it?" she asked, her voice tentative.

Scott didn't look up. He didn't respond. He just kept working, his focus on the task at hand.

Laura waited for a moment, but it was clear he wasn't going to answer. She felt her chest tighten again. Her next words came out in a rush. "I guess you think I'm just like the others, don't you?"

Scott kept his back to her, not even acknowledging the question.

"I'm not. I really am sorry if I hurt you," she said, her voice quieter now. "I don't ever want to do that."

There was a long silence before he finished with the fish, his hands working mechanically. He handed her one of the cooked fish, still warm, and she took it from him, her fingers brushing his. She wiped her eyes, trying to make eye contact, but he didn't look up. Instead, he turned, and for a brief moment, she thought he might speak, but he didn't.

He paused as if something were on the tip of his tongue, but then, as quickly as the moment had come, he walked away.

Laura stared after him, her heart heavy in her chest. The silence pressed in on her again. She sniffled and wiped at her eyes, but the tears kept coming. They weren't the tears of regret or guilt. They were the tears of something else—something she couldn't quite name.

Her eyes met his for a brief moment before he broke the gaze, kneeling on the ground. His face was blank, unreadable. It made her want to cry harder, but she held it in.

After what felt like an eternity, Scott spoke. His voice was low, distant. "The raft will be finished tomorrow," he said, his words punctuated by the finality in his tone.

And then, just like that, he turned and walked away. Laura's gaze followed him until he disappeared into the woods, the sound of his footsteps fading into the distance.

Her serious face softened for a moment, and another tear slipped down her cheek. She wiped it away quickly, but the feeling lingered, heavy and unspoken. She was alone again, even if she wasn't entirely sure what had happened to make her feel this way.

28

HELICOPTER

Scott worked in the heat of the afternoon, his hands raw from the labor of the last few days. The raft was almost done. One more log to tie in place, one more rope to secure. The water was low, the river running slow, and the raft would float just fine once it was finished. He looped the rope around the last log, his movements quick and efficient. But as his hands pulled the cord tight, he stopped.

There was a sound. Something unfamiliar. A low hum at first, then a steady thrum, a whirring sound like something mechanical. He frowned and straightened, wiping the sweat from his brow, listening harder. The sound grew louder, closer, unmistakable now. A helicopter. His heart skipped a beat, and his mind raced. What the hell was a helicopter doing out here?

He stood still for a moment, his eyes scanning the horizon, trying to make sense of it. The trees ahead were thick and dense, but beyond that—nothing. He had no idea who would be out there, but the fact that the sound was growing louder meant it was coming closer.

Scott took a breath and started running. His boots hit the ground hard as he moved toward the riverbank. The raft, half-finished, was forgotten. There was no time for that now. He had to get their attention. He had to do something.

The helicopter cut through the sky, its blades slicing the air with a sharp rhythm that echoed down to the forest below. Inside, the two men sat silently. The pilot had his hands on the controls, his eyes on the trees ahead. The observer sat beside him, staring through binoculars, scanning the forest floor below. They were searching for any sign, any clue that would lead them to her.

"Keep your eyes peeled," the pilot said quietly, his voice almost lost to the sound of the engine. "We're getting close."

The observer nodded, but his eyes didn't leave the binoculars. He scanned the river below, the way it twisted through the woods, the way it disappeared into the distant tree line.

The helicopter hovered just above the treetops, following the river's path with precision. It was a perfect vantage point, but there was no sign of Laura. The observer shifted in his seat, squinting as they passed over another section of the river.

On the ground, Laura heard it before she saw it. The sound of the helicopter was unmistakable, loud and deafening in the quiet of the forest. She stood up, shielding her eyes against the sun as she searched the sky.

For a moment, she wondered if it was a mirage—if it was just the heat or something in her mind—but the noise grew louder, and soon she saw the blur of the helicopter cutting through the sky above. She didn't know if they were looking for her. She didn't know if they even knew she was here. But she knew they were getting closer.

Scott had reached the riverbank now, his boots sliding on the rocks as he waded into the water, his legs sinking into the cool, fast-moving current. His heart was pounding, his chest tight with the effort. He couldn't let this chance slip by.

He raised his arms high, waving them with everything he had, hoping against hope that they would see him, that they would understand what he was trying to do. His throat was dry, his breath coming in short bursts, but he kept waving, kept shouting, even though he wasn't sure if they could hear him.

The observer on the helicopter shifted his binoculars, scanning the riverbank below. The trees rushed by, the river snaking its way through the landscape like a living thing. But then—he saw something. A figure standing in the river. A man, raising his arms. The observer's eyes narrowed. There was something desperate in the man's movements, something that made him take notice.

"Pilot, look down. There's someone in the water," the observer said, his voice sharp. "We've got to get a closer look."

The pilot nodded and adjusted the controls, angling the helicopter lower to get a better view. The blades churned the air, but Scott didn't flinch. He kept his arms up, waving, trying to catch their attention.

Laura had watched Scott run, her eyes following him to the river's edge. She hadn't known what to think—did he see something? Was he trying to stop them? She didn't know, but the sound of the helicopter was still echoing in her ears.

She turned her gaze upward, squinting against the sun as the helicopter passed directly overhead. For a moment, she saw the shadow of it passing over her, a massive, dark shape against the bright sky. And then it was gone, lost beyond the trees.

Scott's arms ached, but he didn't lower them. His eyes were locked on the helicopter, which seemed to hang just above the river, moving slowly, methodically. It was almost as if they hadn't seen him, as if he was invisible. He felt the frustration rise in his chest, but he didn't stop.

He took a deep breath and shouted once more, his voice raw with the effort, his throat burning with every word. But the helicopter didn't respond. It simply passed over, continuing on its path along the river.

As the helicopter began to pull away, Scott felt his heart sink. His arms dropped slowly, his body slumping with the weight of defeat. He had tried, but it hadn't worked. The helicopter was gone, and he was standing in the river alone, the sound of its passing already fading into the distance. He let out a long, shuddering breath, and for a moment, he stood still, frustrated, the water rushing around him, the sound of the forest returning to its quiet hum.

29

_—·—_

WE LEAVE TOMORROW

S cott emerged from the dark, his figure barely visible in the soft glow of the fire. He walked straight to the small fire pit where he'd laid out the quail to cook. His hands were rough, and he moved with the same precision, the same single-mindedness that marked every task he set his mind to. He didn't speak, just set to work.

Laura sat by the fire, watching him, her thoughts running through her head like a fast current. The quiet between them was thick with the things left unsaid. Finally, she broke the silence.

"Did you see the helicopter fly over today?" she asked, her voice quiet, but carrying the weight of something that had been bothering her.

Scott didn't look up, didn't even seem to acknowledge her. He just kept working, his fingers deftly pulling at the quail's feathers, stripping them with careful movements. He didn't want to talk. He didn't want to say anything at all.

"Yes," he muttered, as if the word didn't matter.

Laura nodded to herself, though her mind was far from calm. She watched Scott's broad shoulders work, the muscles moving beneath his shirt, his hands steady as he gutted the bird. She didn't know why she still tried. She didn't know why she thought words could break through the silence that had settled between them.

"It flew right over me," she said, her voice trailing off, almost as if she were speaking to herself now.

Scott's eyes didn't meet hers. He just nodded once, the barest acknowledgment.

"Do you think they saw you or the plane?" she pressed, though she had a sense of what the answer might be.

"I wish," he replied, his voice low, clipped. The words were empty, as though they were no more than a reflex, something to fill the air between them. He was done talking, it seemed.

Laura was silent for a moment. The only sound was the crackling of the fire, the hiss of the bird roasting over it.

"Are you finished with the raft?" she asked after a while, her voice uncertain, as if the answer might change something.

"Yes," Scott replied, and that was all. His focus was on the bird, turning it carefully, making sure it cooked through. His hands moved without thought, like a machine that knew its purpose.

"Good," Laura said, though she didn't feel good about it. She just needed to say something. She needed to fill the space that was growing more uncomfortable by the second.

She shifted uncomfortably, her eyes dropping to the ground as she fumbled for words. "It's not easy being honest about everything these days," she said softly, more to herself than to him. She cleared her throat and continued, "I'm sorry I had to lie to you at first. I was afraid that you wouldn't like me if you knew the truth. Now it doesn't matter because you seem to hate me anyway."

Scott didn't respond. He didn't look up. His hands were steady, his face unreadable in the dim light. He simply continued working, his silence heavier than anything he could've said.

Laura swallowed hard, trying to push past the lump in her throat. "I missed my flowers today," she said, the words slipping out before she could stop them. "Are they all gone?"

Scott didn't answer. He just kept working, but Laura could feel his attention shifting, just slightly. He was listening.

She thought about that for a long moment. "I guess it's a gift I have," she said. "To make myself... feel unwanted wherever I go. Or maybe it's a curse."

Scott didn't reply, but his silence felt different now. It wasn't just the absence of words—it was the absence of judgment, of rejection. He was listening, and she could feel that. She needed to say it all. She needed to let it out.

"My father's an airline pilot," she continued, her voice low. "I never really saw much of him. My mother's only mission in life is to socialize among our neighborhood, trying to make everyone believe we were wealthier than we were."

She paused. "Money is the key to her happiness. My father earned more than enough for me, but never enough for her. She talked so badly about him when he was gone."

Laura rubbed her eyes, a tiredness settling in her chest. "She told me the only reason she married him was because she was pregnant with me. Because of me, she had to settle for him. Mom's parents weren't wealthy—they were and are still happy, though. She would tell me from day one that it's just as easy to love a man with money as it is to love a man without."

Scott listened. He didn't speak, but she could tell he was hearing her. She wasn't sure if it mattered anymore, but it was all spilling out.

"My father was always hopelessly attracted to my mother," she went on, the words flowing without thought now. "She uses that attraction daily to get her way. My father isn't home much now because he's beginning to realize how disillusioned he was in the first place."

Laura leaned forward, her elbows on her knees, her face in her hands for a moment. "He and I would get along very well when we were together. He taught me how to fly, how to drive. He'd take me to my horse riding lessons and watch the whole time. He always told me I was as beautiful as my mother."

Her breath hitched, and she wiped a tear from her cheek before continuing. "I think he hoped that I would somehow turn out to be a better person than she was."

She swallowed hard. "When I went away to college, I met a boy. Greg. He reminded me of my father. Someone my mother would obviously disapprove of. We had an animal-like attraction. I wasn't an angel, not by anyone's standard."

She paused. "Greg wanted to be a musician. Though it was obvious, yet cute in a way, that he would undoubtedly fail. He sucked. But he was honest, sincere. I loved him more than anyone on Earth. Those three months with him were the happiest of my life. Until I got pregnant."

Scott hesitated, his hands stilling for a moment as the words hit him. But he didn't say anything. He just looked at the bird on the fire.

"Greg wanted it," she said, her voice cracking slightly. "I wanted it, too. My mom didn't. She made me promise not to tell my father and forced me to have an abortion."

Laura paused, the memory heavy in the air. "She took me to the clinic herself. Afterwards, she sent me home in a cab because she was late for her bridge club. Three years went by now."

She wiped another tear away, not caring anymore. "I think of my baby, what he would've done with his life. It was a boy, they said."

Scott didn't move, but he was listening.

"Greg left me after trying to deal with all of it. We were never the same again. He said he was scared to make love with me, for fear if I became pregnant again, I'd kill it."

Laura lowered her head, a bitter smile on her lips. "Just a few days ago, my father found out. Now he hates me for not confiding in him, but most of all, he hates my mother for making me do that against my will. They're getting a divorce after 26 years of marriage."

She looked at Scott then, though his face was unreadable. "The last words my mom said to me were, 'This is all your fault, you little slut... don't ever talk to me again.'"

Scott was done with the food. He picked up the quail and brought it to her, wordlessly, his movements slow, deliberate.

"We leave tomorrow," he said, his voice flat. He didn't stop to look at her, just turned and walked into the night, disappearing into the darkness without another word.

Laura watched him go, her heart heavy in her chest. She felt the words still hanging in the air between them, unspoken, unresolved. She dropped her head, the tears falling freely now.

30

HARD TO BELIEVE

L aura sat in the chair, her eyes fixed on the office walls, their beige surface dull and unremarkable. The light from the window outside was fading, casting long shadows that seemed to stretch across the room. The silence pressed against her, and the clock on the wall ticked steadily, marking time she could hardly bear. She had been here before, in this room, in this place. But it all felt distant now, as if the person who had lived through it no longer existed.

Dr. Johnston cleared his throat, his voice cutting through the quiet. "Laura?"

She blinked, as if waking from a dream, and turned her gaze to him. He was looking at her expectantly, waiting for something. But the words she needed to say were stuck in her throat, caught somewhere deep inside her.

"I couldn't believe how disconnected he became," she said finally, her voice softer than she intended. "I really thought I knew him."

Dr. Johnston didn't respond right away. Instead, he reached for the drawer in his desk, pulling it open with a creak that echoed in the room. The sound was sharp against the stillness. He sifted through a stack of papers before pulling out a file, thick with notes. He flipped it open, checked the contents quickly, and then placed it in front of him on the desk.

Laura's eyes followed the file as it landed. She felt a strange unease in her chest. The file was so clinical, so detached. Just like everything that had happened.

Dr. Johnston glanced at her, his brow furrowing slightly, but his tone remained steady. "I suppose he didn't communicate with you much until the rescue."

The question lingered in the air. Laura didn't speak right away. She wasn't sure how to respond, or if she even wanted to. The words felt too heavy, too real. But she had to answer.

"Actually," she began slowly, her fingers tapping nervously on the armrest of the chair, "he did, in many ways."

Dr. Johnston's eyes narrowed slightly, as if he hadn't expected that answer. He set his pen down and leaned forward, his interest piqued. "What do you mean?"

Laura hesitated. It wasn't easy to explain, not the way she felt about it. She could still see Scott, his face unreadable, his presence so distant. It was as though something inside him had shut down, and no matter how hard she tried to reach him, she couldn't break through the wall he'd built.

She swallowed, gathering the words that had been waiting inside her for so long. "The next day... he just seemed happy," she said, her voice almost lost in the weight of it. "Happy that it was the day he would be floating me out of there. It's almost as if... as if he intentionally tried to hurt me by ignoring my feelings."

She paused, her throat tight, the air in the room heavy with the truth of what she had said. She could still feel the coldness in him, the way he had been so wrapped up in his own mission, his own resolve, that he hadn't noticed how much she was hurting. He hadn't noticed how much she needed him to see her, to understand that the world had shifted beneath her feet, and she didn't know how to stand anymore.

But Scott hadn't looked at her. Not really. He had only seen the raft, the way out. He had only seen what was in front of him, what he had to do. And nothing else had mattered.

Dr. Johnston's gaze softened, but he said nothing. He just nodded, as if absorbing what she had said, allowing the silence to stretch out between them.

Laura looked away, her eyes drifting back to the window, but she no longer saw the fading light outside. What she saw was Scott, standing in the distance, moving further away from her with every step he took, as though he were walking into another world altogether, leaving her behind.

31

ALL ABOARD

Laura woke to it, blinking against the brightness of the new day. For a moment, she just lay there, her body heavy with the weight of the last few days. Her eyes wandered slowly around the camp, noting the absence of Scott. The place that had become home was now empty, save for her belongings neatly packed and placed on the riverbank—everything in its place, as if it had all been carefully arranged by someone who no longer cared to stay.

There was a peach and some berries waiting for her breakfast, just as there had been every day. But today felt different. Today, there was no Scott to sit beside her and share the silence. There was no companionship, no unspoken understanding between them. He was gone.

The sound of water rippling against the shore caught her attention. At first, she didn't recognize it—just a faint murmur in the distance—but as it grew louder, it became clear. It was Scott, singing some ridiculous song again. His voice was a little off-key, but it carried through the morning air, light and unburdened, the way he had always sung when he was trying to ignore something.

She watched him as he came into view, standing at the stern of a makeshift raft, struggling to control the clumsy vessel. The current was stronger than he expected, and the raft began to veer off course, drifting dangerously close to the rocks. With a grunt, Scott jumped into the river and, with a rope tied to the raft, hauled it back to the bank. He made it, finally, pulling the raft up just in time to avoid smashing into the shore.

Laura laughed.

"Do you really expect me to get on that piece of crap?" she called out, her voice light, but edged with something else—maybe regret, maybe just the need to say something.

Scott didn't answer her. Instead, he finished tying the raft to a tree and began moving her things onto it with a quiet efficiency. He was already lost in his own thoughts, focused entirely on the task, ignoring her words.

"Isn't it a beautiful day?" he asked, his eyes on the raft, his face still as unreadable as it had been for the last several days.

Laura didn't answer him right away. She looked at the raft again, taking in the sight of it, the way it bobbed against the current, the way Scott worked with it as though it was just another part of the landscape, something to be tamed.

"Happy to get rid of me finally, huh?" she said, the words slipping out before she could stop them.

Scott didn't acknowledge her question. Instead, he glanced at her, his expression hard to read, and then asked, "Have you gone to the bathroom yet? We're not pulling over."

"No, not yet," she replied, her tone dry.

"Well, you might as well. I'm going to get one more thing."

She nodded and walked off into the bushes, the quiet of the woods closing in around her. When she returned, Scott was standing there, holding a makeshift stretcher, crafted from sticks and cloth, his face set in determination.

"Are you ready for your big trip?" he asked, the hint of a smirk playing at the corner of his mouth.

Laura couldn't tell if he was being serious or sarcastic. "Can't wait," she said, her voice sharp with irony.

Scott tried to lift her onto the stretcher, his hands awkward and careful. "Okay," he said, trying to sound gentle, "I'm going to try not to hurt your leg, but I need to get you onto this thing."

She stiffened as he reached around her, lifting her body slightly to position the stretcher beneath her. The movement made her wince.

"So far, so good. Are you okay?" Scott asked, his voice low and cautious.

"Yes," Laura answered, her teeth gritted.

"I'm going to have to lift your broken leg now. It'll probably hurt. At the same time, I need you to lift your other leg to get the stretcher under you. Okay?"

"Okay," she replied through clenched teeth.

Scott slowly, carefully, lifted her leg, the movement pulling a sharp cry from her lips.

"Ouch!" she gasped, her breath catching in her throat.

He continued, his hands steady as he slid the stretcher beneath her. "Lift your other leg," he instructed, his voice soft but firm.

She managed to move her other leg, the pain shooting through her like a thousand needles.

Finally, he set her leg down gently, and she let out a small sigh, the worst of it over.

"There," Scott said, his voice almost reassuring, "that wasn't so bad, was it?"

Laura's laugh was sharp, full of sarcasm. "Ha ha," she said, her eyes squinting as if the pain was still fresh.

Scott didn't respond to her, just picked up the stretcher and began moving it toward the raft. "That leg really needs some attention," he muttered, his eyes focused on the task at hand.

"Yeah," she said bitterly, "it would be nice to get to a real doctor."

Scott stopped, his face darkening at the edge of her comment. He dropped the stretcher to the ground, his eyes narrowing.

"Sorry," he said, almost apologetically. "It slipped."

"Sure it did," Laura muttered under her breath, but her words held no real bite. She just wanted to get it over with.

Scott picked her up again, lifting her carefully, and began dragging her toward the raft. She was heavier than he'd expected, and the weight of it made him grunt as he moved.

"You're too heavy," he said, his voice gruff.

"Ha ha," Laura replied, a weak attempt at humor.

They reached the raft, and Scott carefully dragged her onto it, making sure she was seated before moving to the next task.

"There's a hole in the seat," she said, eyeing the makeshift chair with skepticism.

"I know," Scott answered. "That's there just in case you have to go while we're on the river."

Laura shot him a look, half-exasperated, half-amused. "Great. I guess you thought of everything."

Scott didn't reply, just motioned for her to adjust her position. "Shift your butt onto the chair."

Laura winced but did as he asked, her body protesting the movement. Once she was settled, Scott placed a life jacket around her neck. The straps bit into her skin, tight and unforgiving.

She looked at him then, really looked at him for the first time in what felt like days. He was already back to work, preparing the raft for the river. His face was set, determined, but the emptiness in his eyes was unmistakable. And for a moment, she wondered how much further he could push himself before he broke. Before they both did.

32

THAT OLD MAN RIVER

The raft drifted slowly down the river, the current steady but strong. Tall trees loomed on either side, their dark branches creating a corridor of green that seemed to stretch on forever. Laura sat still, her body tired but her mind restless. She watched as Scott stood at the front of the raft, his long stick dipping into the water, pushing them forward. His voice cut through the quiet of the morning, rising in a song.

"That old man river," he sang, the words trailing off with the current. His voice was a little rough, but he put his whole body into it. The sound of it filled the air around them, echoing off the canyon walls that surrounded them.

Laura winced, holding her hands over her ears. "Would you stop singing just for one minute, please?" she said, the words half a request, half a plea.

Scott didn't respond right away, but the song died off, and he fell quiet. He didn't apologize. He didn't need to.

Laura looked at him, standing there, his face tilted up toward the sky as if the song still lingered in his mind. She thought about asking him something, anything, but the words stayed stuck in her throat.

She didn't know what she was hoping for anymore. She didn't know what he wanted.

"How long do you think it will take before we reach any sign of civilization?" she asked, her voice soft.

Scott paused, his gaze fixed on the river, and then he answered, his voice casual, like it didn't matter much. "Well, we've got the cruise control set for about seven miles per hour. We should cover about seventy miles before it gets dark. That should get us pretty close."

Laura didn't say anything more, her eyes drifting to the water again, to the trees on either side. The world felt small, the river all that mattered, and everything beyond it, everything she had ever known, seemed too far away to reach.

The raft continued its slow journey down the river.

Later, Scott brought the raft to the bank, finding a spot to beach it for the night. He was silent, as was Laura. They didn't speak much now. It was as if they both understood something unspoken. Their time together was coming to an end, and neither of them knew how to say goodbye.

The fire crackled between them, flames flickering as Scott worked over it, preparing the fish. Laura sat on the ground, her face lit by the glow, watching him move. The crackle of the fire was the only sound, except for the occasional whisper of wind through the trees. It was as though the world itself was holding its breath.

Scott didn't look up. He kept his back to her as he worked, his movements careful and measured. It was something familiar. But there was a distance between them now, a quiet that neither of them knew how to fill.

Later that night, after dinner, Laura lay on the ground, staring up at the sky. The stars hung high above them, scattered across the heavens like forgotten dreams. It was a clear night, the kind that made everything else seem small and insignificant in comparison.

Scott came into her view, his shadow falling across the sky. She could see his figure against the stars as he crouched down beside her.

"Are you sleeping?" he asked.

"No," she replied.

Scott lay down next to her, the ground hard beneath them, but neither of them cared. There was nothing to say now, nothing left to say.

"You know," Scott began after a while, his voice softer than usual, "if that helicopter was looking for your plane, they may have people on foot looking for you as well. They'll probably see the smoke from the fire tomorrow, and you'll be on your way."

Laura didn't answer right away. She just lay there, staring at the sky. Her mind wandered back to the crash, to the way everything had been before—when it had all seemed like a mistake, a series of unfortunate events strung together.

"Why didn't you make love to me?" she asked, the question tumbling out before she could stop it. "Is it because I'm so ugly, or because I'm so stupid?"

Scott stiffened beside her. His voice was quiet, almost harsh. "Laura."

She turned to face him, her eyes dark with questions. "I want to know the truth. I hurt you, and I never meant to."

Scott hesitated, then answered, his words slow but steady. "I don't know. You're by far the most beautiful woman I've ever met." He paused, his voice almost absent, like he wasn't really saying the words to her but to something far away. "Like tonight... the way the firelight makes your face glow. You're beautiful, Laura."

She didn't know how to take it. His words were kind, but they felt distant. "So if you find me so desirable," she said, her voice quiet, "why not let me be your first?"

Scott didn't answer for a long time, his face turning toward the fire. "I can't," he said finally. "I can't explain it to you. I'm the one that's crazy. Not you."

Laura wanted to argue, to tell him it didn't matter, that they were here, now, together. But she didn't. She just lay back, staring at the stars again, trying to make sense of what he had said.

"You're just nervous," she said after a moment. "It's okay, you know."

Scott turned toward her, his eyes searching her face. "I really wanted to," he said, "but only when I thought you wanted me for me. When I thought your crash was a freak accident, I thought maybe fate brought us together. Maybe it did, but I'm not sure."

Laura frowned, turning her face to him. "So it's because you think I'm crazy?"

Scott's voice was softer now, almost sorrowful. "Laura, it would be selfish of me to let you stay with me. No matter how much I want to. Your leg needs real attention. Now."

A beat passed between them. He kept talking, almost as if he needed to say it, to explain himself. "Anyone that's determined enough to take their own life has the potential to use that determination to get through another day. Whenever someone is in that low state of mind, things can only get better. Nothing good or bad lasts forever."

Laura opened her mouth to speak, but he cut her off. "You've got the tools to succeed in that world. You shouldn't be weak like me, hiding out here."

"I don't think you're weak," she said quietly. "It takes a lot of strength to do what you've done. To live out here, away from it all."

Scott shook his head. "No, Laura. I've made stupid choices, and I have to deal with them. I'm the fool."

She reached for him, her hand resting gently on his arm. "Why can't you come back with me?"

Scott's eyes softened for a moment, but he pulled away. "I'm happier out here," he said. "This is where I belong. Somebody has to help all the lost pilots find their way back after crashing in my woods."

Laura squeezed his arm, her voice pleading now. "Could you give it a try? Just for a little while? Come home with me. Maybe you'll like it. Maybe I need you there."

Scott looked down at her, his eyes troubled. "I'll think about it. But get some rest. Tomorrow's going to be a big day."

She smiled faintly, but there was no joy in it. "Tomorrow, we may have to say goodbye."

Scott turned his face to the sky, his body still, his thoughts far away. After a moment, he moved closer, brushing a tear from her cheek with the back of his hand.

"We can't stay together like this," he whispered, his voice low, almost a confession. "I'll always be with you, Laura. You know where to find me."

He touched her chest, just above her heart, and then leaned in to kiss her. It was gentle, brief, like the brush of a breeze. Laura closed her eyes, letting the sensation of the kiss settle in her bones. He pulled away slowly, his lips lingering for just a second longer.

"Go to sleep," he said softly, his voice barely more than a murmur.

She smiled, her eyes still closed. The two of them lay side by side, staring up at the stars. And for a moment, there was nothing but the quiet sound of the river, the crackling of the fire, and the night sky that held them both, far from everything else.

33

THE RESCUE

The dogs were the first to hear it. Their noses sniffed the cold morning air, catching a trace of something distant, something faint but familiar. They barked and howled, their voices rising in the dawn, sending ripples across the river. A group of men followed behind them, each holding the leash of a dog. The search party moved in a tight, coordinated line, the dogs tugging forward, their noses pulling them closer to the scent.

The riverbank was silent except for the shrill barking, the low growl of the animals as they tracked something. The scent was growing stronger, leading them to a small clearing where the remnants of a camp lay scattered on the ground. The smell was fresh, but it wasn't just any scent. It was the smell of someone who had been alone for too long.

Laura woke to the noise. At first, it was nothing but a faint barking in the distance, a sound too distant to recognize. But then it grew louder, closer, insistent. She blinked, trying to clear the fog from her mind. For a moment, it felt like the world was spinning around her, the edge of the river, the trees, the fire she had left behind the night before. But when the realization hit her, it hit hard.

The dogs were coming.

Her heart skipped. Her breath caught in her chest. She shot up from the ground, her body stiff and sore. The camp was empty. The raft was gone. The place where Scott had slept was untouched, the fire cold.

She stood up on trembling legs, her eyes wild, searching the clearing for any sign of him. Her mouth felt dry as she opened it to call out, her voice catching in the back of her throat.

"Scott?" she whispered at first. And then louder, more frantic, "Scott!"

She screamed his name with all the desperation she had left, her voice raw from the effort. It was the only thing she could do. She had no idea where he had gone, or why. But the silence that followed her scream made her feel more alone than ever.

The search party heard her scream, clear and desperate, echoing off the trees. The dogs stopped barking, their noses twitching as they froze. The men held their breath, their bodies tense, listening. The dogs pulled forward again, their paws tearing at the earth, their sense of purpose sharp now, leading them toward her.

The search party leader took a step back. His hand went to his radio, his voice steady but urgent. "Alpha One, this is ground team Charley. I think we found her."

The transmission crackled through the static. A long pause followed, and then the faint sound of confirmation.

The dogs surged forward, their handlers close behind. The leader stayed for a moment, watching the trees ahead, making sure the path was clear. Then, with a final glance toward the team, he followed.

Laura sat on the ground, her legs pulled tight to her chest, her face hidden in her hands. Tears streamed down her cheeks, but she couldn't make herself stop. She had no energy left, no hope. Not after everything that had happened. Her mind was fogged with the noise of the dogs, the crash, the fire, and now this — the thought that Scott had simply vanished, that he had left her behind.

She didn't even hear the search party approach until the dogs stopped pulling, their bodies tense and still, sniffing the air. Then, the men were there, kneeling beside her. They asked her questions, checked her condition, but all she could do was stare into the distance, too numb to answer.

The leader crouched in front of her, his voice kind but firm. "Are you Laura?"

She looked up at him, her eyes wide, empty. She tried to smile but it felt wrong, like a lie. "Yes," she managed, her voice barely above a whisper.

"Are we glad we found you," the leader said, relief in his tone. The rest of the team moved around her, their hands gentle as they worked to apply first aid, checking her wounds, ensuring she was stable. They asked her more questions, but she didn't respond. She couldn't.

Her thoughts were still with Scott. Her eyes scanned the horizon, hoping, praying that he would emerge from the trees, his raft somewhere just out of sight. But there was nothing. Only the sound of the helicopter growing louder as it approached.

The helicopter came in low, hovering above the riverbank. Its blades chopped through the air with a deafening roar, drowning out the cries of the dogs. A rescue basket was lowered from the rope, swaying in the wind, waiting to carry Laura away from the wilderness. She didn't resist.

She couldn't.

The men carefully positioned her on the stretcher, securing her tightly. Her broken leg throbbed in pain, but she barely noticed. Her eyes searched again, one last time, for any sign of Scott, but he was gone.

The rope began to pull her up. Slowly, inch by inch, she was lifted into the air, the stretcher creaking under her weight. The helicopter swayed as it tried to keep its position, the pilot working hard to steady the craft against the gusting wind.

Up she went, higher and higher, until the ground below her was just a patch of green, the trees shrinking away beneath her. The world seemed to tilt, the perspective of the riverbank warping as the helicopter swung around.

The side door of the helicopter opened wide, and Laura was pulled inside, the warmth of the interior a stark contrast to the chill of the morning. The door slammed shut behind her with a heavy thud. The helicopter spun in a quick 180-degree turn and started its flight down the river, the trees below becoming nothing more than a blur.

She looked out the window, her heart pounding. Below her, the river curved around the bends of the land. The helicopter's roar was deafening, but it didn't matter anymore. She was leaving the wilderness behind. She was leaving Scott behind.

Her thoughts turned dark, the tears still fresh on her face as she stared out into the distance. She didn't know what was next. She didn't know what would become of her or Scott, but for now, the only thing she could do was hold onto the hope that they had both survived, in some way, even if only for a little while longer.

34

A HYPOTHESIS

Dr. Johnston broke the silence. "He just disappeared?"

Laura nodded, her eyes still fixed on a point beyond his reach. Her voice came out soft, distant. "I woke up, and he was gone."

The doctor leaned back in his chair, his fingers pressing together in a thoughtful steeple. "How did that make you feel?"

"Sad. Very sad." Her voice cracked as the words tumbled out, and she blinked, trying to keep her composure.

A tear slid down her cheek, and she wiped it away quickly, her breath shallow. "I guess I'm crazy."

Dr. Johnston didn't look at her, instead, his eyes dropped to the folder in front of him. The pen was put down, and he rubbed his chin thoughtfully. "No, Laura. You're not crazy. In fact, your case is rather interesting. One of the most interesting I've come across in my twenty-some years of practice."

Laura gave a small, bitter laugh. "Well, at least I'm not boring you."

"No, I find it quite... fascinating," Dr. Johnston said, his tone not quite sympathetic but measured, clinical. "I actually believe you're excessively normal, Laura. You might take things to extremes, yes, but that's not necessarily bad. It's... human."

Laura wiped her eyes again, her hand trembling slightly as she looked up at him. She felt a sharp pang of confusion in her chest, the words not quite registering. "What are you talking about?"

Dr. Johnston leaned forward slightly, his expression softening, but not entirely. "From what I've gathered, from my talks with your parents and what you've told me today, your greatest fear seems to be... loneliness."

Laura's heart seemed to stop for a moment. "Loneliness?" she echoed, the word heavy on her tongue.

"Yes," Dr. Johnston continued. "Your actions, your decisions—seem to be motivated by a fear of facing the world alone. It's common, especially for young people. I think, perhaps in your mind, you wonder what you can do to please your father so he won't leave, so he won't abandon you." He paused, looking at her with eyes that seemed to pierce right through. "Maybe you tried to please him by taking an interest in this career, by learning to fly."

A beat passed, and then he added, "You've also mentioned your mother. Your behavior sometimes mirrors hers, as you described it. In some way, you seem to be trying to gain her approval, hoping she'll stay—hoping she'll accept you, despite everything she's said to you."

Laura's hands clenched the arms of the chair. She wanted to interrupt him, to scream that he didn't know what he was talking about, but the words wouldn't come. She stared at him in disbelief, her body still, as he continued.

"And with Scott, you told me that you did everything with him, anything, even when you needed him most... and he wasn't there."

Laura's breath caught in her throat. "Can we stop now?" Her voice shook. "I get it. I've been sitting here listening to you talk, and the most interesting case of your career is just that I'm... lonely?"

Her lips curled into a wry smile, though it didn't reach her eyes. "I guess I'm cured now, right? Now that I know I'm just lonely and weak like everyone else. My mother, my father, Scott. It doesn't matter anymore what they think of me. They don't have to worry about me anymore." She laughed softly, but there was no joy in it. "I'm so happy now."

Dr. Johnston shifted uncomfortably in his chair, but he kept his voice even. "Okay. I'm glad you're feeling better."

He pressed a button on the intercom without looking at her. "Yes, Doctor?" came the voice from the other end.

"Can you send a nurse with a wheelchair to help Laura back to her room?" he asked, his tone suddenly light, as though the conversation had shifted.

"Yes, sir. Just a moment."

Dr. Johnston gave Laura a small, reassuring smile as he began to look through her file again. Laura sat there, feeling the strange emptiness of the room press down on her. A nurse appeared shortly after, a wheelchair in hand. Laura used her crutches to push herself into the chair, her leg now properly cast, but still heavy with the weight of the words she couldn't shake.

Dr. Johnston didn't look up. He continued flipping through his file as though nothing had happened.

"Thanks," Laura muttered, her voice small.

"You're welcome, Laura. Good luck."

The nurse began to back the wheelchair toward the door, but Dr. Johnston's voice stopped her.

"Oh, one more question, Laura, if I may?"

Laura frowned. "Yes?"

The nurse stopped in her tracks, unsure. Dr. Johnston gestured for her to wheel Laura back into the room.

As they returned to the desk, Dr. Johnston's demeanor shifted slightly, his eyes narrowing, his voice taking on a different tone—one that made Laura's chest tighten with sudden unease.

"I was just wondering," he said, slowly, as though the words were being measured, "how you were planning to do it this time."

Laura blinked. "What?"

She looked at him, puzzled. She hadn't expected this. Dr. Johnston's gaze was steady, unreadable.

"How you were planning to... end it all. Take your own life. Commit suicide," he said, his voice calm, matter-of-fact. "I just wanted to know, so we'll know when your room will be available."

Laura's mouth went dry, and the world seemed to shift beneath her. "I—I don't know what you're talking about."

Dr. Johnston didn't flinch. Instead, he put the file down, stood up, and walked toward her. His voice was softer now, but still firm. "Yes, you do. Just say it."

"Say what?" Laura whispered, her heart racing.

"I don't want to live," Dr. Johnston said. He said it so easily, so bluntly, as though it were the simplest thing in the world. "Just say it. I know it's true."

Laura turned away from him, her face crumpling with the weight of the words. "Please stop."

"Not until you say it," he pressed, his voice rising slightly.

"Will you just shut up?" Laura snapped, her breath quickening, a surge of anger fighting against the fear crawling up her spine. She tried to push her wheelchair away from him, but Dr. Johnston stepped forward, grabbing the wheel.

"Say it!" he demanded.

"Let me go!" Laura cried out, her hands gripping the arms of the chair as she tried to push herself away.

"Laura!" His voice was insistent, unyielding. "Say it!"

Laura screamed, a raw, broken sound. "Leave me alone!"

The room fell silent for a long moment. Laura's chest heaved with the weight of her emotions. She cried—harder than she had in days, in weeks, maybe longer. Dr. Johnston stood motionless, watching her.

A nurse entered, concerned, but Dr. Johnston gestured for her to leave them alone. She hesitated, glancing at Laura, but then she stepped out, closing the door softly behind her.

Laura wiped her eyes with the back of her hand, her voice cracking as she spoke. "Please?" she asked, so quietly it was almost a whisper.

Dr. Johnston didn't respond at first. He just stared at her, his expression unreadable.

"I'm afraid I can't do that," he said finally, his voice low.

"Why not?"

He sighed, the sound heavy in the quiet room. He walked over to the desk, picked up a folder, and threw it down in front of her. He knelt beside her, looking her straight in the eyes. "Whether you know it or not, you really don't want to die."

Laura shook her head slowly, her lips trembling. "Yes, I do."

Dr. Johnston shook his head. "When I spoke with your mother, she admitted she wasn't very supportive of your needs. She may have been too concerned with her own. She said she wanted to work on that... by whatever means possible."

"So, it's a little late," Laura muttered, her voice flat.

Dr. Johnston didn't respond right away. He continued, speaking carefully. "I asked her if she could remember one time when you two connected emotionally, if she'd ever seen you cry and offered support."

"Never," Laura whispered, her throat tight.

"To my surprise," he said, "she said she'd only seen you cry once, since you were an infant. Five years ago, actually. You were in the living room, watching the news. You were alone, but when she came in to call you for dinner, she found you crying." He paused, looking at her. "Do you remember that, Laura?"

Laura sat still, staring at Dr. Johnston. Her mind was fogged with confusion, trying to make sense of the disorienting conversation. The weight of his words hung in the air, the silence between them thick, almost palpable. He had just dropped a bombshell, but her response was instinctive, defensive.

"I have no idea what you're talking about," she said quietly, her voice trembling just a little, though she tried to disguise it.

Dr. Johnston's gaze softened slightly, but his words were as firm as ever. "You asked her to come join you and listen," he repeated, as though piecing together a puzzle he'd just begun to solve.

Laura felt a chill. She wanted to turn away, but her eyes were fixed on him now. He was saying things she couldn't understand, truths she didn't recognize. He went on, almost in a whisper, as if recounting a painful memory, "She said you were so emotionally affected as you listened to the story of a local young person that committed suicide. You both cried, for an hour, in each other's arms. Do you remember?"

Her heart skipped. The image of her mother—so distant and cold most of the time—holding her, comforting her, felt alien. She blinked, shook her head slowly, as if trying to shake off the weight of his words.

"I don't remember," she whispered.

Dr. Johnston didn't pause. He reached for a photograph on his desk, placing it in front of her. "Do you recognize this person?" he asked quietly, his eyes never leaving hers.

Laura looked at the image. Her breath caught in her throat. She knew that face. Scott. The name rose to her lips, but it didn't make sense. Not now. Not like this.

"Hey, that's Scott!" she said, her voice rising with panic. "Where did you get this?"

Dr. Johnston said nothing, just let her gaze linger on the photograph. The headline read, Young Man Found Hanged in the Woods. Laura's breath caught, her fingers trembling on the edge of the paper.

"No," she whispered. "Scott's not dead. I just saw him a couple of days ago. He—he's alive." Her voice cracked, but the words came out anyway, a desperate plea to hold onto the truth she had known.

Dr. Johnston remained calm. "Laura, Scott's body was discovered in the woods by a couple of hunters about five years ago. The state police arrived on the scene and took these photographs."

His hand extended toward her, and she slowly reached for the stack of photos, flipping through them numbly. Each image was worse than the last. The twisted form of Scott, hanging by a rope, his lifeless body swaying in the wind. Her throat closed as she stared at the photographs, unable to comprehend what she was seeing.

"This can't be true," she muttered, a tear slipping from her eye.

Dr. Johnston's voice was steady, but there was a quiet sorrow in it, as though he had to say it out loud for both of them. "The police report concluded that Scott committed suicide. He hung himself, Laura. He's been dead for five years."

Laura shook her head vehemently, as though if she denied it hard enough, it would go away. "No," she said again, louder this time. "No, I just saw him. He is alive. I can show you. I—I talked to him."

Dr. Johnston's gaze never wavered. "No, Laura," he said softly, but firmly. "The incident was the talk of this small town for weeks. You heard about it on the news. You knew who he was. You even heard his story."

Laura could feel her world crumbling around her, the foundation of everything she knew cracking and shifting.

"No," she whispered again, her hands shaking as she looked up at him. "I don't believe you."

Dr. Johnston sighed, as if preparing himself for the hardest part of the conversation. He reached for a stack of newspaper clippings and handed them to her. As she took them, the weight of each word in those headlines felt like stones pressing down on her chest.

Scott Allen, 21, Found Hanged in Local Woods.

Her mind reeled. Her hands began to tremble uncontrollably as she flipped through the clippings, each one telling a version of the same tragic story. Her heart clenched as she came to the obituary, a simple, stark farewell to the boy she had known, the boy she had seen just days ago.

"Then who was it that saved me?" she whispered, the question a fragile, broken thread. "Someone who looked like Scott? Someone pretending to be him?"

Dr. Johnston's expression softened. "Nobody, Laura. You saved yourself."

Her head jerked up, confused. She opened her mouth to argue, but no words came out.

Dr. Johnston continued, speaking with the calm authority that had characterized their entire conversation. "It's my theory, Laura, that after you crashed your aircraft, you went into shock. When left untreated, shock can cause all sorts of temporary psychiatric disorders. In your case, it triggered a rare form of schizophrenia. You thought you were with someone. You saw someone. You felt someone. But all along, it was just your mind, trying to protect you."

Laura's eyes filled with tears, but she couldn't look away from him. "It was all in my head?" she asked, her voice barely a whisper.

He nodded. "Your subconscious saved you from yourself, Laura. Deep down, you didn't want to die. You just wanted to feel connected. You wanted to belong."

"But what about the camp?" she asked, her voice trembling with the weight of her confusion. "The splint on my leg, the raft?"

"You applied the splint yourself. You were a Girl Scout once, remember?" he said. "Everything else? The camp? The raft? It was all in your mind. Your subconscious created an imaginary world to keep your body from further harm."

Her head was spinning, the truth still slipping through her fingers like water. "If I could make up my own world," she muttered to herself, "then why was Scott here? Why not someone else—someone famous, like Brad Pitt?"

Dr. Johnston gave her a small, understanding smile. "Because, Laura, your mind gave you what you needed. It gave you the one person you needed to feel like you weren't alone. Scott. He was the one who, in your mind, was supposed to save you."

She wiped her nose with her sleeve, looking down at the floor. "I don't understand," she said quietly.

"You only bonded with your mother once, during that story on the news about Scott," Dr. Johnston said gently. "That's when the two of you cried together, for a whole hour. That's when you felt connected."

Her chest tightened. The memories of that night, so far removed from everything now, felt distant, strange. But they were real. "I don't remember who it was that killed himself," she whispered. "I don't remember."

Dr. Johnston leaned in, his voice soft but filled with an unspoken weight. "In your attempts to please the world, Laura, you left out the most important person—yourself. You have to take the painful journey inside, to find out who you truly are. Only then will you be able to connect with others in a way that truly matters."

She sat there, trying to digest everything, trying to make sense of the wreckage that was her life. Dr. Johnston handed her a tissue.

"I don't know how I'll ever believe this," she said quietly. "All of it. The world I lived in. The feelings I had for Scott. It was real to me."

Dr. Johnston's eyes softened. "It's okay to keep those memories, Laura. They're a part of you. They're a step forward. A positive one."

He hugged her then, a brief embrace, but one that felt genuine. A tear slid down Laura's cheek, the weight of everything finally sinking in. She had no answers yet, no way of understanding fully what had happened, but for the first time in a long while, she felt like the world was not a stranger to her. She was not alone anymore.

35

— • —

I'M SORRY

D r. Johnston wheeled Laura down the long, sterile corridor, the sound of the wheels turning against the floor the only noise between them. The smell of antiseptic was sharp in the air, and the harsh overhead lights flickered now and then, adding a stuttering rhythm to the otherwise silent space.

Laura's mind was a thousand miles away, trapped in memories that refused to stay silent. She closed her eyes, and images of Scott began to surface—vivid, like shards of glass.

She saw him laughing, his face soft with joy, as they sat on the porch at sunset, the air cool against their skin. The light had been golden then, and it hadn't mattered that the world outside had been dark and heavy. She could still hear his voice. "You've got the heart of a pilot, Laura," he'd said, his eyes shining with something she couldn't quite place.

The wheelchair bumped lightly over a crack in the floor, pulling her back into the present. The corridor stretched endlessly before them. The faint hum of distant voices, muffled and far away, whispered along the walls.

Dr. Johnston pushed her gently into a room. The door opened with a quiet sigh, revealing a space filled with people.

The room was warm, alive with voices, but there was an air of reverence, too. Relatives and friends crowded in, their faces strained, their smiles stiff as though they didn't quite know how to show their relief. A banner hung against the far wall, a simple declaration of love—WE LOVE YOU LAURA—but it felt almost too much for her to take in all at once. It was overwhelming. She had been absent from this life for so long, locked away in her mind, that it now seemed a world too full, too loud.

Her father approached her first. His broad frame loomed above her as he leaned down to kiss her forehead, his eyes glistening with unshed tears. She saw the tears well up in his eyes, saw how tightly he held them back, as though he had feared this moment might never come.

"Who taught you to fly like that?" he asked, his voice thick. He didn't need to explain. She knew what he meant.

Laura's eyes blurred with tears, and she swallowed hard. The lump in her throat was large, impossible to ignore. "I'm sorry about your plane, Dad," she managed to say, the words coming out too softly, too heavy. The crash, the wreckage, the devastation—she hadn't meant for any of it to happen. She never had.

Her father squeezed her shoulder, his grip firm, a mixture of pain and something softer. "It's you I care about, kiddo," he said quietly, his words cutting through the fog in her mind. He wasn't angry anymore. He wasn't disappointed. He was just... relieved.

Before Laura could reply, her mother stepped forward, her movements hesitant, as though unsure of the right way to reach out. She stopped just shy of Laura's chair, her hands shaking at her sides. The room fell into a heavy silence, and Laura could feel the weight of her mother's gaze, like a heavy hand pressing down on her chest.

Her mother finally spoke, her voice cracking, raw. "I'm sorry," she said, her words hanging in the air between them. "I was so wrong."

Laura looked up at her mother, searching her face, her heart pulling with a tenderness she hadn't known could exist between them. She had always wanted her mother's approval, her love, but it had never come easily. Now, it was all laid out before her—her mother's tears, her apologies—and something in Laura's chest loosened.

"Me too, Mom," Laura whispered, her voice breaking. She wiped her eyes and reached out, her arms open, desperate for the comfort she had been too afraid to ask for. "I love you, Mom."

The crowd in the room, quiet until now, let out a soft cheer, as if they had all been holding their breath, waiting for this moment. For the first time in a long while, the weight on Laura's heart felt a little lighter.

Someone handed her flowers, the soft, sweet scent of them mingling with the faint hospital air. She took them in her hands, the petals delicate against her fingers.

As she gazed down at the bouquet, the memories of Scott flickered through her mind again, the flowers he had given her—his wild, unrestrained gestures, his smile when he handed them to her, as though he had just given her the world. The flash of those memories took her breath away.

"Thank you," she said, her voice barely above a whisper, the words aimed at no one in particular but to everyone in the room at once. It was gratitude, yes, but it was also something more—a quiet plea for forgiveness, for understanding, for the chance to find her place in this new world that was now hers to navigate.

The flowers in her hands were soft, like memories, fragile but persistent. They would fade eventually, as all things did, but for now, she held onto them. And for the first time in what felt like an eternity, she wasn't alone.

36

I'M GOING TO BE FINE

The first light of dawn crept through the small window, casting soft, pale stripes across the sterile room. The air smelled faintly of antiseptic and something colder, the kind of cold that settled in the bones of places where time moved too slowly. Laura was sleeping, her face peaceful for the first time in what felt like ages. Her breath was steady, her body still.

Then, with a sharp intake of breath, she sat up in the bed, the suddenness of it making her chest tighten. Her eyes scanned the room, blurry from sleep, but it didn't take long for them to focus.

Scott.

He stood there in the closet, his back to her, rummaging through her things. His movements were slow, deliberate, as if he hadn't meant to disturb her.

"Scott?" Laura's voice cracked as it broke through the quiet of the room.

Scott turned around, his eyes wide and surprised, as though he hadn't meant to wake her. His face softened into that familiar, comforting smile that made her heart ache.

"I'm sorry," he said. "Did I wake you?"

Laura blinked, her eyes still half-closed with sleep, but her mind raced, trying to grasp what was happening. "What are you doing here?"

Scott gave a small shrug, a gesture that was almost sheepish. "I found that wish I thought I lost," he said. "Just wanted to drop it off before I left."

He stepped closer, as if moving on a secret cue, and looked down at her. "How is your leg?"

Laura didn't answer right away. She just stared at him. This was impossible. This had to be impossible. But he was standing right there, in front of her, his messy hair falling into his eyes, just the way it always did.

Scott met her gaze with a steady calmness, as if he had known she would ask the question. "I guess you know now why I was in the woods," he said, his voice lower, more serious than before.

Laura swallowed hard, her throat dry. "They said you killed yourself," she whispered, as if just speaking the words might make them real.

Scott didn't flinch. He simply nodded, his face twisting with a quiet regret. "I told you I was the fool," he said. "I didn't realize why I was made to stay out in the woods. They told me you held the memory of my stupidity, that you were going to try something similar. They wanted me there to talk you out of it."

Laura's breath caught in her chest. "You mean..." She trailed off, unable to finish the thought.

Scott's smile was sad now, but there was a softness to it that made Laura's heart ache. "I did what I could," he said, his voice barely more than a whisper. "Now, they're letting me move on. I'm one of the lucky ones, Laura. They don't like it when people take their lives, you know?"

Laura only stared at him, unable to speak, her mind too tangled in confusion. She couldn't understand it, not all of it, but she could feel it—the truth of it—deep in her chest.

Scott took a step back, his eyes meeting hers one last time. "Listen," he said gently. "I was told to tell you that you're going to have a long and wonderful life."

Suddenly, a bright light flashed through the window, slicing through the dim early morning like a beacon.

Scott turned to face the light, a quiet finality in his movements. "Well," he said, looking back over his shoulder, "that's it. That's my ride."

Laura's voice broke through the haze, desperate, filled with something she couldn't name. "Scott!" she called out.

Scott stopped and turned back toward her, his eyes soft, filled with something she couldn't quite reach.

"I love you," she said, the words tumbling out before she could stop them, before she even realized how badly she needed to say them.

Scott stepped closer to her, his warmth filling the space between them. He kissed her, a soft, fleeting press of lips, and when he pulled away, his smile was bittersweet.

"I love you too, Laura," he said, his voice thick with emotion. "But there will be others. I can promise you that. And not as dumb as me."

He turned, walking toward the light, his movements slow and steady, like he knew where he was going. "I'll see you again, Laura. But not too soon, okay? Now, wake up."

And with that, he stepped into the light, disappearing from her sight.

Laura's chest rose and fell as if she had been holding her breath the entire time. She blinked rapidly, trying to clear the fog that had settled in her mind, and suddenly, the world around her felt unbearably still.

"SCOTT!" she shouted, her voice rising with a frantic desperation. Her eyes darted around the room, her heart racing in her chest. But she was alone.

"SCOTT!" she called again, her voice trembling.

Her cry was cut short as a team of nurses entered the room, their eyes wide with concern.

"Are you okay, dear?" one of them asked, her voice gentle but firm.

Laura looked around the room, her breath quick and shallow. "Did you see him?" she asked, panic creeping into her voice.

The nurses exchanged glances, their faces unreadable. "See who? It's okay, dear," another nurse said softly.

"You had a dream," Nurse One said, smiling as she gently tucked Laura back under the blankets. "That's all."

Laura's eyes welled with tears as she tried to hold onto the fading memory of Scott, but the room felt so real, so full of warmth and light that she couldn't let it go.

"It was so real," she whispered, almost to herself.

Her gaze drifted to the nightstand beside her bed, and her breath caught in her throat. There, lying next to her bed, was a wild flower—a peach-colored bloom with delicate petals. And beside it, a handful of berries, still wet with dew, along with a crude drawing of a turkey.

"Oh my GOD," Laura gasped, her chest tightening. She reached for the flower, the drawing, the berries, but her hands shook.

Tears began to fall, silent at first, but then they came harder, a flood of emotions she hadn't expected, hadn't prepared for.

Nurse One looked at the other nurses, a silent command passing between them. "Get Dr. Johnston on the phone," she said.

As Laura wept, the nurses gathered around her, their hands gentle, their voices soft.

"Please," Laura managed between sobs, "get my jacket."

The nurses hesitated, exchanging uncertain looks, before one of them turned to fetch the jacket.

"It's in the closet," Laura urged, her voice sharp with a sudden urgency.

Nurse Two began moving toward the closet, but before she could reach it, the phone in the room rang. Nurse Three picked it up, her voice low and professional.

"It's Dr. Johnston," she said, holding the phone out toward Laura.

Laura took the phone, her hands trembling as she held it to her ear.

Dr. Johnston's voice came through the line, groggy and distant. "Are you okay, Laura?"

Laura didn't answer right away. She was still in shock, still trying to make sense of what had just happened.

"Scott was just here," she whispered, her voice barely audible.

Dr. Johnston didn't respond immediately. "It was just a dream, Laura," he said gently. "Just a dream."

Laura wasn't listening anymore. She dug through the pockets of her jacket, fingers shaking.

And there it was. The flower—a squashed white bloom, just like the one Scott had handed her that night by the water.

Her breath caught in her throat. The memory of their dance, the way he had smiled at her, the way he had given her the flower—it all flooded back at once.

She opened the top pocket, and there it was—folded neatly, a small piece of paper, its edges frayed with time. She unfolded it slowly, and her heart stopped.

"I wish I was alive."

The words were written in Scott's messy handwriting, each one a quiet plea that she had never understood until now.

Tears flowed freely now, joy mingled with grief. She laughed, her chest trembling with emotion. "I'm going to be fine," she whispered, her voice thick with the weight of the moment.

Dr. Johnston's voice came through again, soft and concerned. "Are you going to be okay?"

But Laura didn't answer at first. She didn't need to. She held the note to her chest, her face wet with tears, her heart lighter than it had been in years. "I'm going to be fine." Laura smiled as she disconnected the call.

The nurses moved around her, preparing her breakfast, offering her medication, but she didn't see them. She only saw Scott, and the light he had left behind.